Pig and the Blue Flag

for April

The Seabury Press, 815 Second Avenue, New York, New York 10017

Text copyright © 1977 by Carla Stevens
Illustrations copyright © 1977 by Rainey Bennett
All rights reserved. No part of this book may be reproduced or
transmitted in any form or by any means, electronic or mechanical,
including photocopying, recording, or by any information storage and
retrieval system, without permission in writing from the publisher.
Printed in the United States of America.

Library of Congress Cataloging in Publication Data

Stevens, Carla.   Pig and the blue flag.
"A Clarion book."
Summary: Pig just hates gym until a game of
"Capture the Flag" proves his value to his teammates
and to himself.
[1. School stories] I. Bennett, Rainey. II. Title.
PZ7.S8435Pi   [E]   76-58384   ISBN 0-8164-3192-2

PIG and the Blue Flag

by Carla Stevens

illustrated by Rainey Bennett

A Clarion Book
The Seabury Press · New York

Pig liked school.
He liked everything about school
except for one class
on Monday, Wednesday, and Friday.
Gym.
Today was Monday.

"Time for gym," said Otter, his teacher.

"Yay! Yay! Yay!" everyone shouted.

"Yippee!" yelled Raccoon.
She looked at Pig.
"Why don't you yell too, Pig?"

"I only yell 'yippee' for something I like.
  I don't like gym."

"I *love* gym." Raccoon said.

"That's because you are good in gym.
  If I were good,
  I'd love gym too," Pig said.

"Today we are going to learn
   to turn somersaults," Otter said.
"Bend down.
   Put your head between your legs.
   Give yourself a push
   and over you go."

"That's easy," Raccoon said.

She turned a somersault.

Then Muskrat turned a somersault.

Then Rabbit and Weasel.

And Possum and Squirrel and Beaver.

At last it was Pig's turn.
He put his head between his legs
and gave himself a push.
Nothing happened.

"What are you doing, Pig?" Raccoon asked.

"I'm stuck," Pig said.

"I'll give you a push." Raccoon pushed.
But Pig did not turn over.

"You don't try hard enough," Raccoon said.

"Yes I do," Pig answered.

"If you try, you will be good at something."

"What?" asked Pig, still upside down.

"He's just too fat," Squirrel said.

Otter blew his whistle.

Pig got up.
"Whew!" he said.

Gym was over for Monday.

On Wednesday, gym day, Otter said,
"Everyone get in a circle.
You must catch the ball
when it is tossed to you.
If you drop it,
you are out."

Raccoon stood next to Pig.

"Hold out your hoofs.

Get ready to catch the ball," she said.

Pig held out his hoofs.

Otter tossed the ball to Raccoon.

Raccoon tossed it to Weasel.

Then Weasel tossed it to Rabbit.

Pig's thoughts turned to chocolate cupcakes.

That morning his mother had put two
in his lunch box.

Suddenly, Squirrel tossed the ball to him.

The ball hit Pig's hoofs,
then bounced on the ground.

"You're out, Pig!" called Otter.

"Butterhoofs! Butterhoofs!" said Squirrel.

"Pig, you didn't even try to catch the ball.
What's the matter with you?" Raccoon asked.

"Gym is what's the matter with me," Pig said.
And he sat down under the tree
and tried to think about lunch
until the bell rang.

It was Friday, gym time again.

"Today we are going to play a running game,"
  Otter told the class.

"It is called 'Capture the Flag'."

"Yay! Yay!" everyone shouted.

"On no," Pig groaned.

"I get a pain in my side when I run."

"There are two teams and two flags,"
  Otter explained.

"The point of the game
  is to get the other team's flag
  and carry it back to your own territory."

"Raccoon, you are the captain of the red team,"
Otter said.
"Possum, you are the captain of the blue team
and you choose first."

Possum called out, "Rabbit!"
Rabbit ran over and got behind Possum.
Rabbit was the best runner in the class.

Then it was Raccoon's turn to choose.
She chose Weasel.
Weasel ran over and stood behind Raccoon.
He could run almost as fast as Rabbit.

Possum called out, "Beaver!"
Then Raccoon picked Squirrel
and Possum picked Muskrat.
Finally, everyone was chosen but Pig.

"You can have Pig," Raccoon said.

"No thanks," said Possum.
"You take him."

"Oh, all right," Raccoon said.
"Come on, Pig."

Pig sighed.
"I'm always the last one picked."
He got in line behind Squirrel.

"You must wear a ribbon
so that we know which team you are on.
The red team wears red ribbons," said Otter.
"The blue team wears blue ribbons."
Otter passed out the ribbons.

Pig looked at his red ribbon.
It was not long enough to fit
around his middle.
Raccoon went over to Pig.
"Here, Pig. Let me tie it on your tail."

"It is supposed to go around his middle,"
Squirrel said.

"It doesn't matter, Squirrel."

"Yes, it does," Squirrel said.
"He looks funny."

"Listen everyone!" called Otter.

"I have drawn a line across the center
of the meadow.

Now the meadow is divided into two territories.

One for the blue team, one for the red team.

At the far end of your territory is your flag.

In one corner is a big circle."

"What's the circle for?" Raccoon asked.

"The circle is your prison," Otter said.
"When someone runs onto your territory,
 you must try to tag him
 and put him in prison
 before he captures your flag."

"No one will tag me if I stay on my own territory,"
 Pig said to himself.

"How do you get out of prison?" asked Squirrel.

"Each time someone is caught,
   he holds a former prisoner by the paw
   to make a chain," Otter said.
"You can free all the prisoners on your team
   if you can tag the last one
   at the end of the chain
   without getting caught yourself.
   Do you all understand the rules of the game?"

"Yes! Yes!" everyone cried.

"Then let's start," Otter said.

The blue team ran over to its territory.

The red team ran over to its territory.

"Ready, get set, GO!" yelled Otter.

Suddenly, everyone began running.
Rabbit ran across the line
onto the red team's territory.
She ran fast.
She wanted to be first to capture the red flag.
Weasel ran after her
but he couldn't catch her.

"Tag her Raccoon!" he yelled.

Raccoon blocked Rabbit and tagged her.
"Got you!" she said. "You're a prisoner.
Come with me."

Raccoon led Rabbit to the prison circle.

"Hooray! We got the blue team's best player!

Don't let anyone free her, Pig," she called.

"Now let's try to get *their* flag.

Come on, Weasel!"

Pig stayed near the prison.

What if someone tried to free Rabbit?

What could he do?

Weasel ran across the line
onto the blue team's territory.
He ran very fast.
"I can get that blue flag easily!" he shouted.

But suddenly someone grabbed him.
"You're caught!" said Possum.
"Go to prison."

Soon everyone was a prisoner
except Possum and Raccoon and Pig.
"Free us! Free us!" the prisoners
on both sides yelled.

Raccoon ran over to Pig.

"Listen, Pig. I know how we can win,
but you must help.
I will get Possum to chase me.
Then you run across the line and get the flag."

"Me?" said Pig.
"I can't run fast.
Besides, I get a pain in my side
when I run."

"Possum can't run fast either," Raccoon said.

"What if Possum catches me?" asked Pig.

"It doesn't matter," Raccoon said.
"It's only a game."

Everyone was still yelling.

Raccoon ran across the line.

Possum chased her.

Raccoon ran faster.

Possum was right behind her.

Suddenly Pig began to run.

He ran onto the blue team's territory.

"Hey, watch out for Pig!" yelled Rabbit.
"Catch him, Possum!"

Possum looked over at Pig.
Then he looked at Raccoon again.
Should he chase Raccoon
or should he chase Pig?

Pig kept running.
He ran faster than he ever had in his life.
He ran all the way to the blue flag.
He picked it up.

Possum saw Pig with the flag.
Possum began to chase Pig.

"Oh no," said Pig.
"I'll never make it back home.
Never."

All the prisoners on the blue team were yelling,
"Tag Pig! Tag Pig!"
Possum was gaining.

"Everyone is counting on me," thought Pig.
"Only a little farther
and then I'll be safe."

But Possum was coming closer and closer.

"Faster, Pig! Faster!" yelled Squirrel.
Pig could feel something.
Was he tagged?
He thought he would keep running anyway.

43

He reached the line.
He was safe on his territory at last.

Suddenly everyone was around him.
Pig held out the flag.
"Here's the flag, Raccoon."

"You made it!" the red team yelled.
"We won! Hooray for Pig!"

"That was good running, Pig," Squirrel said.

"Here, Pig," said Possum. "I tagged your ribbon
 but I didn't tag you."

Raccoon gave Pig a friendly pat.
"See what happens when you try?"

"I could never do that again
in a million years," Pig said.
"Never."

"Line up everybody," Otter called.
"Gym is over for today."
Everybody lined up.

"Otter," said Pig.

"Yes, Pig."

"When are we going to play
Capture the Flag again?"

"On Monday, if it is a nice day," Otter said.

"Good!"

"Did I hear you say GOOD, Pig?" asked Raccoon.

Pig did not answer,
but he nodded
just as the bell rang.

More about Capture the Flag

Possum and Raccoon had only four players
on each team.
It is much more fun to play Capture the Flag
when the teams are big.
When there are many players,
each team should have a guard to guard the flag,
and a guard to guard the prisoners.
Only the first prisoner
must stay within the prison circle.
The prisoners hold hands to make a chain.
The more prisoners, the longer the chain.
All the prisoners are freed at once
when a member of their team
tags the last person on the chain
without getting caught.
It is easy to free prisoners,
but it is hard to do what Pig did—
capture the flag and win the game!

A WEEK IN OCTOBER

ELIZABETH SUBERCASEAUX

A

WEEK

in

OCTOBER

a novel

translated by
Marina Harss

OTHER PRESS · NEW YORK

Translation copyright © 2008 Marina Harss

Copyright © 1999 Elizabeth Subercaseaux

Originally published in Spanish as *Una semana de Octubre* in 1999 by Editorial Grijalbo, S.A. de C.V.

Aria lyrics on page 166 from *The Bohemian Girl*, opera composed by Michael Balfe, libretto by Alfred Bunn.

Production Editor: Yvonne E. Cárdenas
Book design: Natalya Balnova

This book was set in 11.5 pt Bembo by Alpha Graphics of Pittsfield, New Hampshire.

10 9 8 7 6 5 4 3 2 1

Library of Congress Cataloging-in-Publication Data
Subercaseaux, Elizabeth.
    [Semana de octubre. English]
    A week in October / by Elizabeth Subercaseaux ; translation by Marina Harss.
        p. cm.
    ISBN-13: 978-1-59051-288-3
    I. Harss, Marina. II. Title.
    PQ8098.29.U25S4613 2008
    863'.64—dc22

                        2007051357

to John Hassett

Quintín has found and read my manuscript.

—— ROSARIO FERRÉ
The House on the Lagoon

Contents

THE ANNOUNCEMENT

I only noticed the deep silence in our shabby room when I became aware of the fluttering wings of a fly trapped between the lampshade and the light bulb. There was no noise from the street below. It was as if the outside world had disappeared. Lionel lay on his back staring up at the ceiling, completely serene, so quiet and still that it was almost as if he weren't there. He had just put out his cigarette, and the white smoke hovered in the air. I was sitting beside him with my legs drawn up and my chin resting on my knees.

"It's strange how things happen," I said.

Lionel said nothing.

"Don't you think this is strange? Sometimes I wonder whether everything is preordained. What do you think? Perhaps the two of us were meant to spend these hours together making love. When I think about it, I get shivers. It would mean that all of this is predetermined and that there are no real choices in life. I would rather believe that, within certain limits, we are free to make decisions for ourselves and we control our own destinies. What do you think?"

Still no answer.

I turned toward him. . . . He lay still, staring up at the white ceiling. His eyes were open, fixed, unchanging, without the slightest glimmer or expression, extinguished. He made no sound, and his face had taken on the quality of marble.

This is how his life came to an end. Without a sound, without a sign, without the slightest warning. Like a mosquito moving from here to there.

At first I thought my bad luck had rubbed off on him, that I had become a kind of King Midas in reverse, killing everything I touched. I felt as responsible for his death as I have felt at times for my own approaching demise. But now I realize that even though this illness is the prelude to my own end, it was not the cause of my lover's death. Lionel's death had its own origin, the previous Saturday in my garden when I saw a strange old woman pissing next to one of the plum trees.

On that morning of Saturday, October 9, as I was turning the soil in a spot where I was about to plant some tomatoes, I had a strange sensation, like the one I felt the day we buried my grandmother at the Molco cemetery. The essence of things had changed; it was as if the plum trees Clemente had planted, the leaves of the ferns, the soil I had just turned so carefully, and even I myself, had been invaded by a new presence. I looked at the sky and noticed that it had gone dark; a mass of dense, black clouds closed in overhead, and a moment later the world was enveloped in a heavy silence. "How strange, it's only eleven in the morning, there must be a storm coming," I thought, trying to contain my increasing anxiety. I noticed that all the living things around me had stopped breathing. The air was thick, like a hazy midsummer afternoon. I felt as if I had awakened in a hot, static dream, in which I was trapped in the crushing stillness of a sudden and inexplicable night.

Suddenly I was sure that someone else was in the garden with me. I turned my head, and saw a tall, bony old woman, dressed in black rags. She had materialized out of nowhere and was squatting as she pissed next to the trunk of a plum tree, only a few feet away from me. She did not look at me. She just went on as if I did not exist. My eyes were fixed on the gushing liquid. It was a clear, continuous stream. The pale gold torrent fascinated me; in my mind, the piss of death should have been a viscous green liquid that emitted a fetid odor that stayed with you forever. The old woman just went on pissing ever so calmly, without any sense of urgency or shame. It was as if she would never stop. I knew that all I could do was wait for her to finish.

"This is it," I thought, my mind racing, a whirlwind of dark thoughts crisscrossing like bullets in my brain. "This old woman has come for me. There's no doubt about it. When she's finished she'll say, 'Well, Clara, the rubber band has been stretched to the limit, and I will not return alone to the pastures where eternity sleeps.' That's it, my time has come, this is the end of the line. Where is it written that one will die in bed, or in a hospital after struggling for two weeks with a serious illness? There are no set conditions for death. 'This fell sergeant, Death, is Strict in his arrest,' Shakespeare wrote. He is indifferent to the age of his victims. People die when and where they least expect it: in the bathtub, while driving, while giving a speech. Or while reading *Dubliners*, like my father. How and when one dies is of the slightest importance; the difficult part is what comes after: waking up and not knowing what to do or where to go; feeling that there is no ground beneath one's feet, that there is nothing but air all around; finding oneself in a place where one sees no one and hears only an internal rumbling, a place where there is no way to distinguish between day and night, because neither light nor the absence of light exists. And knowing that one will be there, in that state, forever. . . ." This last thought made the little hairs on the back of my neck stand up.

As these thoughts went through my head, the woman looked up at me, brushing an oily lock of her hair off her forehead. Her gaze was familiar. I realized with horror that her eyes were my own. . . . How terrifying, she was me. . . . Something very bad must be about to happen, this is the sign. At that moment I did not know what it could be, or what the horrible woman who stared at me with my own eyes had come to tell me. The most natural thing was to assume that this was how my illness had decided to announce my ultimate demise, but a little voice told me no, the old woman had come to warn me about something else.

What she was actually announcing was my lover's death, but, of course, at the time there was no way to know this because my lover did not yet exist. Or rather he existed for many other people, but not for me.

And then to my astonishment the old woman vanished, as unexpectedly as she had appeared. The sky began to brighten; my heart rang in my ears as I hurriedly picked up my gloves, which I had dropped, as well as the hoe and the small rake I had bought a few days earlier. I ran into the house. As I crossed the dining room I stopped in front of the mirror next to the door. I was still me, Clara Griffin, and nothing had changed. Here was my pale, thin face, the same face as on every other day, my black eyes, my full, sensual lips. . . .

Perhaps I had not been visited by death, and perhaps it is wrong to believe in such strange visions. Once I was back inside my bright, comfortable home I felt safe. Not that I really cared for that house; I never had. Or rather, I had never been truly happy there. Now that I think about it I don't know if I have ever been truly happy anywhere, but I know that in that house I always felt as if I were living in a space that was not my own. Everything there was beautiful, but it was hushed and insipid, a house where good taste and harmony reigned, where everything had its rightful place, and everything was painstakingly clean. Nothing there was ugly, but nothing belonged to me. It was a place without a soul. The furniture, the paintings, the carpets, the antique furniture, everything had been chosen by Clemente. Even before these items had arrived at our house, their placement was already determined. It was as if even before those rooms were built—designed for the measured, precise life that Clemente loved and I found depressing—Clemente had already decided what objects he would select and where he would place them. There were the two Flemish stuffed chairs on either side of the chimney, the English desk next to the window that had once belonged to a president, the beautiful Regency bookcase against the back wall that Clemente had bought in Valparaíso, and the blue Sèvres vase on the table in the vestibule. And there was the Coromandel screen, once the property of a French millionaire who had decided she did not want to die in Chile and had returned to her old house in Saint Jean de Luz. And the Queen Anne mirror Clemente had given me for our tenth anniversary. "This mirror is a rare piece from the early eighteenth century," he had said as he handed me the delicate lacquered object, a mirror with a small drawer underneath, large enough for three compacts and two brushes. "The mirror of our discontent," as he later christened it. Perhaps I would have felt that this beautiful object was truly mine if Clemente hadn't said, when I mentioned I would like to keep it in our room to use as a vanity, that our room was not the appropriate place for such a piece and we would keep it on the side table near the dining room door.

When Clemente was a child his paternal grandfather lived in a Tudor mansion, which still exists. The house filled his adolescent imagination with dreams. The old man was a millionaire "in dollars," a specimen so rare in Chile at the time that they could be counted with the fingers of one hand. He detested Clemente's mother and called her "the foreigner." He loved to tell people that his son could have married anyone but instead had chosen this unknown Dutch girl. Clemente was ten years old when his father died, and his mother, who had become hard and taciturn, did not let him visit his grandfather after that. Clemente, who adored the old man, never again saw him or anyone else from his father's side of the family. He spent the rest of his childhood in a depressing apartment with his widowed mother, who was filled with bitterness toward the society that had excluded her. He continued to dream of his grandfather's mansion and way of life. When he built his own house, Clemente unconsciously settled the score with his mother, who had estranged him from half of his family and exiled him to their dank, gray apartment, which was always filled with the lingering fragrance of cooked cauliflower and wet rags. The smell engulfed him each time he set foot in the place. His mother seemed determined to bask in her misery by being as unhappy as she possibly could and allowing her surroundings—the chipped bathroom mirror, the slimy strips of cloth she used to hold together the putrid pipes, the sagging curtains, the chipping paint on the walls— to reveal her unhappiness. All of this misery conspired against any lingering affection Clemente might have felt for their messy, ramshackle home.

Many years later, when she criticized him for building such a luxurious, expensive house, he expressed his feelings about his childhood—in his own way, of course: "I need to live in harmony with my sensibilities, Mother." The main qualities of our home were equilibrium and light: perfectly calibrated illumination, ample spaces, high ceilings, bright walls. It was the polar opposite of the smelly hovel he had grown up in. The paintings were lit indirectly by special spotlights Clemente had built into the corners of the rooms. In the winter, the fireplace was lit at four o'clock, every day. Bathed in the glimmer of the flames, the beautiful white marble Buddha in the living room came to life. In the summer months the house was filled with the syrupy sweetness of jasmines. And beyond the windows lay the carefully tended garden, surrounded by ferns, and beyond that, the kitchen garden I had planted with my own hands. That was before I knew that my death had a preordained date. This was where, earlier that morning, I had experienced the hair-raising vision of the old woman.

"I know it's impossible, I know there's no escaping an illness like mine, but I wish there were something I could do to pull away from its reach, something that would allow me a release from myself," I had said one day to Clemente as we stood on the terrace, watching the darkening sky. "Why don't you try writing?" he answered, without hesitation, as if he had been thinking about it for a long time. I was surprised that he came up with the idea so casually, without hesitation. He had stumbled upon the one thing I had always wanted to do: to write a novel. When I was young, I had written a few stories and I told myself that one day I would be a great writer. But the impulse never went beyond believing in my own delusions. I have never been a disciplined person and I've spent years not knowing what I want and not living the way I want. Perhaps now that the date and time of my death had been revealed to me, I was ready to write. But how would I begin?

{The Notebook}

*C*lemente knew that Clara had been thinking about writing. He was the one who had suggested the idea. One afternoon when they were drinking *pisco* sours[1] on the terrace, Clara had said she wanted to do something that would help take her out of her illness, something that would make her forget herself, because this obsession was going to kill her long before the illness did. She needed air, an escape, a chance to think about other things. "Why don't you write something?" he had said, and Clara seemed taken with the idea.

One night Clemente heard a noise downstairs. He got out of bed. In the kitchen, he opened the drawer where Clara usually kept a flashlight, and found a note-

---

[1] A common cocktail in Chile and Peru, made out of *pisco* (a local brandy), lemon juice, egg whites, syrup, and bitters.

book. It caught his attention. On the cover, written in block letters in India ink, were the words: *A Week in October.* And on the next line, in small red letters: Clara Griffin. It was a notebook of the kind used to keep accounts, thick, with cardboard covers.

Clemente opened the notebook and recognized Clara's pointy, perfectly regular handwriting. He flipped through the pages, and then started to read: "I only noticed the deep silence in our shabby room when I became aware of the fluttering wings of a fly trapped between the lampshade and the light bulb."

". . . I felt as responsible for his death as I have felt at times for my own approaching demise. But now I realize that even though this illness is the prelude to my own end, it was not the cause of my lover's death."

Clemente felt a cold shiver down his back; nothing made him feel more anxious, more powerless, or moved him more deeply, than hearing Clara speak about her illness. In the seven months since the nightmare began she had done so only a few times, but the distressing echo of those words had lingered in her eyes. Every time he looked into them he could hear it all again. As he read on, he came across his name, and that of his poor mother. And what was this crazy story about a woman pissing in the garden? That was something Clara had made up, because there was no kitchen garden behind the house, and he had never planted a plum tree. Nor was it true that all the objects in the house had been chosen by him or that he wanted to live a measured, precise life. How ridiculous it sounded! It was true that he liked to jot down what he did each day on a calendar. It wasn't a diary exactly, more like a record of events. It was also true that his punctuality was a bit extreme, but she was taking it too far when she said that he preferred a "measured" or "precise" life. . . . He was neat. The poverty of his childhood had taught him to look after his few possessions. Clara had grown up with a wasteful father who believed that everything in this world could be given away or gambled at poker; perhaps that was why she liked to make fun of his love for order. But after all, Clara had taken part in the decoration of the house, and she had chosen much of the furniture. She liked their things, or at least he thought she did. Only the screen had belonged to his grandfather. And it irritated him intensely that she described his mother's apartment as a smelly hovel filled with the stench of boiled cauliflower and his mother as a hard, taciturn woman. . . . His mother had suffered from the disdain his grandfather had shown her from the start and throughout her marriage. The old man was a snob and a miser. He had always refused to help her. He blamed her for his son's death. He refused to pay for his grandson's education even though he was and would forever be his only grandchild, since his father had been his only son. Nasty old man. What did Clara know about all this? It was true that his relationship with his mother had never been easy. He loved her and hated her at the same time. He loved her upright, unflinching quality, the way she had given herself a single goal in her widowhood—that he should have a profession—and worked toward it against all odds, courageously, battling against anything in her path. But he hated the bitterness her drive had produced. . . .

What did Clara know of all this?! It was as if he had decided to write about her father, whom she completely idealized and invested with a series of qualities that existed only in her imagination. He knew from what Aunt Luisa had told him that Clara's father was largely responsible for his wife's depression, and he thought the old man probably bore some responsibility for her terrible death. But Clara had always refused to acknowledge this possibility. She adored him and believed all of his lies; she gazed at him through rose-colored glasses, and after his death he became a genius in her eyes. Clemente, on the other hand, had always cordially detested him. He had never celebrated his stupid and irrelevant quotations of Oscar Wilde, and he felt uncomfortable when the old man referred to women thirty years his junior as "tasty-cakes." Though he too could be won over by the old man's wit and his flashes of originality—he did not deny the man's originality—he had found it difficult to tolerate his constant levity. But it would never have occurred to him to write about his father-in-law, especially now that he was dead. Dirty laundry should be kept private. As the story progressed, he felt increasingly disturbed. What hurt him the most was Clara's assertion that she had never been happy. He knew it wasn't true, he was sure it wasn't so, but why had she written it? Was she suffering from the effects of her illness? It must be hard to live with death breathing down one's neck. Perhaps she saw it everywhere. Was this why she had invented the odd story of the stranger's death? Was this a record of Clara's confused thoughts, muddled by her suffering? What was all of this about? A lover? It wasn't possible. She didn't have a lover, she had never had lovers, he was sure of it. Well, almost sure. She wasn't that kind of woman, now less than ever. . . . So what did it mean? Had she started making up names for people she saw in the street the way she used to? It was a silly habit she had picked up as a child.

He pushed the notebook away and stood with his eyes closed. Clara's illness had affected him more than he realized. Their marriage had reached the point when there are no more battles, when one makes love only often enough to remember that one is a couple, and when one sleeps with one's body pressed against the other's back out of habit. When the skin is no longer as firm or as soft as it once was and the body no longer arouses any sensations beyond those inspired by a warm blanket, this body is still your wife's body and it is still true that you once loved her. For some time Clemente's feelings for Clara had been only slightly more intense than what he might have felt toward a sister. And they had no children. The silence that settled between them over the years had nothing to do with children growing older and moving on but rather with the fact that they had already said everything they needed to say, they had long since revealed all their mysteries. Their curiosity had run its course.

When he had met Eliana, Clemente had already become used to living this way, in peace, and following a somewhat monotonous routine. He and Eliana had been lovers for seven years. Clara did not know about Eliana, and Clemente never had the slightest intention of telling her about the affair. He did not know where it was headed or whether he was really in love with Eliana; her insistence that he leave his wife irritated him, but their connection was red-hot. Their bodies seemed to burn through the sheets in the little apartment where they met on Mondays, Wednesdays, and Fridays from seven to ten. They made love two and even three times, and their bodies became an explosion of stars, a conflagration of words, as they went on and on, almost to the verge of unconsciousness, to the point of exhaustion. In bed, Eliana was the apotheosis of sex, and Clemente feared that if he ever married her—of course, he would never do it—those days of salty sweat would diminish in intensity until they became a handful of mechanical kisses and the measured passage of time, just like a dull marriage. . . . Beyond sex, Eliana simply faded away.

The fact was that he would never be forced to make this choice. Literally overnight, his life was so completely transformed that on some mornings, when he looked in the mirror, he saw the face of a stranger.

One night, Clara had emerged from the bathroom, trembling.

"My nipple is bleeding," she had said.

After that, their lives were changed forever. Early the next morning they had gone to the doctor, and Clara's ordeal began: tests, surgery, a breast removed, three sets of ganglia compromised, chemotherapy, tamoxifen. From then on life became stealthy allusions, walking on tiptoes, sideways glances, and the low, hollow rumble of death.

Clemente put the notebook back in the drawer, walked over to the kitchen window, and lit a cigarette. The flame illuminated his face. He was fifty, but looked much younger. His features were delicate, almost feminine. The fine ridge of his nose and the furrow across his brow were his most pronounced, and perhaps most masculine, features. He pressed his nose against the thick glass and let his eyes wander across the garden. It was a dark night, and the walnut tree was hidden among the shadows. A growing sense of worry washed over him. He was almost sure Clara did not know about Eliana, but what if she did? Suddenly the seven years of his relationship with Eliana came crashing down on him with their weight of guilt. The idea that Clara might die tormented him. He needed her to get better so that he could repay his debt to her. Five years, that was all he needed. He couldn't let her go without making amends, or rather he could not let her go and be left behind with this terrible sense of guilt that would not leave him. One morning before going to the office he stopped by the clinic to talk to the doctors. He wanted to hear them say they could extend her life five years, but the doctors had frightened him with their militaristic, warlike language, a dark language he was sure began to kill their patients and the patients' families even before the illnesses finished them off. Clara's tumor had "invaded" part of her lung, and other cells were "colonizing" different parts of her body; her "defenses" were weak and even though the surgery had been "radical" and their "attack" had been the most aggressive that science allowed, the "tumoral invasion" was still growing and continued to "win battles." "What does all of this mean?" Clemente wanted to know. Finally, one of the doctors spoke clearly and told him the truth.

Clara had, at the most, eight months to live, but Clemente had no intention of telling her, and he forbade the doctors to do so. Clara thought her illness was under control and they should let her continue to believe this until it was no longer possible to deceive her. By September, she might be dead. . . . Clemente shuddered. Almost automatically, he opened the drawer and pulled out the notebook, searching for a paragraph he had read earlier: "What she was actually announcing was my lover's death, but, of course, at the time there was no way for me to know this because my lover did not yet exist. Or rather he existed for many other people, but not for me." If this lover really existed, which seemed highly unlikely, Clara must have met him in the last four months. Was it possible that in four months they had become lovers and he had died, and that all this had happened in the midst of Clara's illness? "It's not possible," he thought, and felt a sense of wonder at this story his wife had made up.

TWO FACES ON THE STAIRS

*T*he arrival of my illness was like that of an all-powerful enemy who occupies all the space around him, physical as well as spiritual, or like a black octopus whose firm tentacles invade every corner of existence. But even invaded in this way, life goes on. On the Saturday in question, Clemente had invited a group of people to celebrate the closing of a deal, a building they were developing in Viña del Mar. Two of the guests were friends of his partner Alberto. Clemente had met one of the guests, Lionel Hyde, only once or twice, but Alberto knew him, and he was interested in buying two apartments. . . . "It feels strange to ask you to join us, but I think it would be good for you, it will distract you," Clemente had said to me. Business dinners bored me to death, so I decided to ask my aunt Luisa if she could join us. Aunt Luisa, my father's only sister, was an educated and witty woman who always had something original to contribute to every conversation. I loved to watch people's surprised reactions to the sophisticated irreverence of this old progressive as she expounded on her Sartrian notions; most people were scandalized by her.

But my vision in the garden had distracted me from the dinner that evening. I felt trapped inside of a deep, troubling story. Death never makes an appearance in vain, at random, or because it has time on its hands. That is not its style. When it comes, something changes, something is transformed; the shape of things is altered. When death came to my grandfather, for example, he was younger than I am now; he was forty-two when he died, and I am already forty-six. Aunt Luisa kept her husband's ashes in a sealed urn on her dresser. He had been a corpulent man with big hands, who exuded passion for life. He loved to travel, and he loved books—he was a doctor, but he could just as easily have been a Greek sailor or a writer like Hemingway. He even looked like Hemingway. Only death was capable of circumscribing that big, bright-eyed, and generous man within the convex walls of an urn that fit into Aunt Luisa's hand.

I had read a story by Paul Auster that haunted my dreams for several nights: somewhere in the French Alps a skier disappeared. He was swallowed up by an avalanche and his body was never found. Many years later his son went skiing in the same spot and discovered a body in the ice, intact and with its eyes open, staring up at the sky, as if the person were still watching the birds flying above him. The man looked more closely, and as he leaned over and peered at the face he had the terrifying feeling he was seeing his own reflection. He examined the face and realized the man encased in the ice was his father, and that his father was younger than he was. It made his heart ache.

With these thoughts fluttering around in my head, I went up to my room. I needed a shower. Halfway up the stairs I stopped in front of my mother's portrait and noticed something about her eyes, which, in the rather poorly executed portrait looked green—in fact, I remember them being quite blue. She seemed to be looking at me differently, as if she knew what had just happened in the garden. Now when I remember this it seems crazy, but the truth is that I heard— or thought I heard—her voice emerging from the painting, a clear, measured voice:

"Beware of the old woman; she'll trick you into thinking that she is you, but don't believe her. She plays games. Tomorrow she could appear under your window making funereal sounds, combing her long gray hair, like a banshee. Don't pay attention, don't let yourself be controlled by the terror she will inspire in you. Run away, Clara, while you still can, far away from her, where she can't reach you with her claws. She's not invincible. You can beat her at her own game, you just have to know how."

Then my mind readjusted to the reality of the silent portrait. I realized that these words coming from my mother's mouth were absurd. She would never have said anything of the sort. She had made no attempt to cheat death. In fact, one could say she had invited death in. She had let herself die, or rather she had been dying her whole life, little by little. I remember her standing next to the window in her room, thin and pale, staring out as if she were waiting for a train. It was never clear what exactly was wrong with her, or perhaps everyone knew all along and no one bothered to tell me, which is likely. They told me she suffered from an illness that made her tired and drained her of the will to live.

Further up the stairs there was a black-and-white photograph of my grandmother at the age of seventy in her garden at Molco. All the serenity that was missing from my mother's portrait poured out of this photograph of my grandmother. She used to talk to the dead and dance *Swan Lake* in the drawing room of the old house.

Many things from that period have disappeared from my memory, and others I have erased. It has always pained me to bring to mind images of my indifferent, depressed mother. I have forgotten the sound of her voice. I can't remember if she ever laughed, and I remember almost nothing of her world, what her room was like, or what furniture she had there. I don't remember her clothes. My father used to tell me that she always wore long gray dresses, but when I imagine her I see only her silhouette, gazing out the window, and her pale face. When I think about my mother my memory becomes thin and full of dark areas. On the other hand, I remember my grandmother very clearly. I remember quite distinctly the night she died. She was not ill, but she had given in to the incurable despair that affects women who have buried a daughter. She had not eaten for days and on that morning she announced she had no interest in drinking water. It was her way of telling the world that she did not want to go on living. After lunch, I went to her room. She was lying in the middle of her big bronze bed, resting on two white pillows, waiting for death to arrive.

"It hasn't come yet," she said when she saw me tip-toe into the room. She looked at her hands as if the exact hour of her death were written there. Then she closed her eyes. I sat in the chair next to the window. There was an echoing of bones in the room. . . . "Death is a solitary matter," she said suddenly, and I understood that she wanted me to leave.

That night I awoke with a start. I had been dreaming about my grandmother. In the dream she disappeared in a puff of smoke from the same bed where I had seen her that afternoon, leaving behind a fragrance of talcum powder and earth. I got out of bed and went to her room in a trance, like a sleepwalker. When I reached her door I pressed my ear against the wooden panel and listened. Inside, I could hear only the silence of an ancient, empty room.

I went in.

The old woman was lying on the bed with her head to one side. There was a strange stillness in the air. Her eyes were open and they stared at the wall, as if death were a painting. Her hands lay across her stomach, her hair was messy, and her thin lips were pressed together in a final grimace.

We buried her the following day, at nightfall, in a cemetery on the slopes of the Trauco, on the side where the wind blows and a cloud of smoke rises from the volcano. When Alamiro and Gilberto lowered the coffin into the ground I had the same feeling as just now, in the garden. It was as if a strange spirit had come over me. It was death inspecting the world to see how it had recovered from its visit, or perhaps it was my grandmother saying to me: "I'm still here."

I took two steps down and again stared carefully into my mother's face. Maybe she and my grandmother were trying to tell me something from the other side. . . . Isn't it said that women are links on a chain and that what happens to the grandmother also happens to the daughter and the granddaughter? Where had I read that? I felt my forehead go cold. Did this mean that I was going to die that very day? At seven thirty, when Clemente returned from Viña del Mar to prepare the cocktail sauce for the shrimp and came upstairs—as he always did—calling out, "Clara, I'm back!," would he find me lying on the bed in a heap? Would he shake me? Would I slide to the floor like a bag of potatoes? Only then would he realize that something serious had happened. But even then he would not be able to accept the worst; he would shake me even more vigorously. "Clara, what's wrong? Clara, talk to me, say something, open your eyes!" Nothing. What could I say? After all, I was dead.

I looked away from my mother's face, overwhelmed by these thoughts. I was furious that she had allowed herself the luxury of inviting death, as if she had nothing better to do. I scrambled up the last four steps to the second floor and picked up the phone in the hallway.

Aunt Luisa's voice brought me back to the present.

"Do you think that death gives you a sign before it comes for you?" I asked abruptly.

"What? Are you all right? You sound like you just finished running the New York Marathon. I was about to call. I don't think I can make it tonight. My legs hurt, and I'm not feeling well. It's just that I'm much too old. I should have gone a long time ago, but don't let me bore you with my complaining. What is this about death giving you a sign?"

"I had a terrifying vision, or some kind of dream, I'm not sure what it was. I was in the garden and suddenly I saw an old woman peeing next to the plum tree."

I described what I had seen.

"It's all in your imagination. Death is far too busy with more important matters; it doesn't have time to go around peeing under plum trees and frightening pretty young women like you," Aunt Luisa said with an uncomfortable laugh. Ever since my diagnosis the very word death stuck in her throat.

"And do you know what the old lady's name was?" she asked, poking fun at my habit of coming up with names for the people I saw in the street.

But I was not in the mood for jokes. "So you're not coming," I remember saying, to change the subject and calm myself. After the visit from the old woman, that evening's dinner was the last thing on my mind. I had no idea that only a few hours later that dinner would become the line dividing what was left of my life into two parts, what came before that meal on the evening of Saturday, October 9, and everything that came after. At the time of my conversation with Aunt Luisa, Lionel did not exist. One week later he would be lying by my side, in the bed in Almarza's tiny apartment, dead. . . . A tiny particle of time is enough to change everything in the most brutal way. . . . A heart attack can leave you staring into eternity. A man you have never met could be traveling in a plane from somewhere in the world and tomorrow, or even before that, he could be locked into your life until the bitter end. A small change that happens in one place can produce a movement far away. If that Saturday I hadn't decided to walk to the market rather than drive—as I usually did—and if I hadn't felt tired after walking fifteen blocks, and if I hadn't stopped at a café to rest . . .

{The Notebook}

*T*wo weeks passed before Clemente dared to look
at the notebook again. He felt he had no right to peek
into his wife's private life. If Clara hadn't shown him
those pages it meant that she did not want him to see
them. The idea that it was a kind of journal that would
never see the light of day gave him peace.

One day he went to the Salvador Hospital to visit
one of his workmen who had suffered a thrombosis. The
grounds seemed empty. Eliana worked in the cardiology department, but he did not see her. He didn't see
any nurses at all, as if the staff were on strike. There
was no one to ask for the room number of the patient
he had come to visit. Clemente went into a room,
thinking it might be his. It wasn't. It was a large room
with a single bed, on which lay a woman of indefinite

age. She looked weak and feverish. She stared into space with glassy eyes surrounded by dark circles. She seemed to be fading away. Her hands grasped a wooden crucifix. When she noticed Clemente she turned to him with a desperate look that either begged him to leave because he had no right to see her last moments of suffering, or begged him to stay with her, not to leave her alone. Suddenly she turned toward the wall and Clemente heard her speak to someone. There was a small mirror next to the bed; a face was reflected there, but it was not the woman's. She was speaking to a ghost. He rushed out of the room and the hospital as if his feet had suddenly sprouted wings, and once he reached the street, he sat down on a bench.

The image of the dying woman stayed with him throughout the afternoon. That night, while Clara slept and despite his reservations, he went down to the kitchen and opened the drawer where he had found the notebook two weeks earlier. It was still there, and Clara had written a few more pages.

Poor Clara, he thought, reading the passage where she described her sickness as a black octopus whose firm tentacles invade every corner of existence. This damned illness is eating away at her soul, he thought to himself, feeling a wave of powerlessness. And it is eating away at me as well. . . . He had always believed that love needed constant movement, that there was no such thing as stationary affection, that love had to go in some direction, up or down, but could never stand still. This belief had helped him justify his relationship with Eliana, because if love ceased to grow, it necessarily began to decline, and a love in decline justifies seeking out another. . . . What a mountain of lies! Now he would give anything to keep Clara by his side, to sleep lying against her soft, malleable back, to feel her familiar thighs and her messy hair tickling his chin; to hear her brushing her teeth over the sink, three times up and three times down, then three times to the side. He would give anything to go back to their life before the illness. . . . The passion had died many years ago, but Clara was his wife and he knew he loved her.

When he reached the end of the chapter he went back and reread the last paragraph. He felt a hot, sour liquid rising in his esophagus. "At the time of my conversation with Aunt Luisa, Lionel did not exist. One week later he would be lying by my side, in the bed in Almarza's tiny apartment, dead." What could this mean? Was this Alberto's friend, the one who had dined at their house a few months earlier? When was that dinner? Sometime in late September, after the eighteenth, of that he was sure because on the eighteenth they had erected a shed on the empty lot in Agua Santa where they were planning to build, and that was where he had seen Lionel Hyde for the second time in his life and invited him to dinner with Alberto and the others. The dinner at his house was after that day. He could check his date book from the previous year. He had surely made a note of it. And Almarza? Did she mean the senator? It was completely far-fetched. But Clemente remembered clearly that during dinner, at some point, Hyde had made a reference to his friendship with the senator; he said that they were both on the board of the fruit exporter Santa Elena. . . . Clara had written: "One week later he would be lying by my side, in the bed in Almarza's tiny apartment, dead." Clemente reread the paragraph three times, shut the notebook with a start and decided to talk to Clara, but then he realized Clara would not only be indignant that he was reading her notebook, but would conceal it. Compelled by an impulse he did not want to recognize for what it was, he decided to say nothing. He put the notebook away in the same place where he had found it and returned to his room.

Clara was still sleeping. Lately, her nights had been calmer, less agitated, and she did not awake screaming as she had in the previous three months. But she was losing weight. She looked thinner, and her skin had begun to turn the grayish hue of cancer. Clemente smoothed the sheet and stood next to the bed for a while.

Then he went down to his office to smoke.

THE TUNNEL

*T*hat day passed in a cloud of anxiety. The apparition of the old lady had unsettled me. I was carrying death in my gut; the last thing I needed was to begin having visions about it. Death is not something we want to elaborate on; the less there is of it, the better.

I remember each thing I did that afternoon between the moment I came back from the market with my bags and the time Lionel Hyde rang the doorbell. I remember taking a nap; Amanda's letter, which Justina had handed me on my return from the market; sobbing in the shower; pulling a black dress out of the closet and then deciding that I would never again wear black, and instead putting on a green dress with white polka dots.

Since Lionel's death I have repeatedly gone over everything I did and practically all the thoughts that crossed my mind on that afternoon until that evening at nine, when the bell rang and Clemente said, "That must be Lionel Hyde. He mentioned he might come early. He just got in from Punta Arenas." At the time I didn't pay much attention and barely heard what he said; now his words come back to me with a painful clarity.

That morning, after a second shower, I went to the market. I decided to walk. Walking calms me down, helps put my thoughts in order. The market was about twenty blocks from our house. I could take a taxi on the way back. I started to walk, like an automaton. A few minutes later I stopped, still in the grips of my apprehension. I could feel the anxiety taking over my body. It was a psychic indisposition, but its expression was physical. My body ached, and I felt the need to stretch my legs until the bones came out of their joints, to stretch my arms until they dislocated from my shoulders. It was a strange sensation, one I had never felt before, as if my extremities were bound and I needed to free them.

I sat down on a bench across from the vegetable stand on the corner of Carmen Silva and El Bosque streets and tried to decipher the cause of my indisposition. It wasn't difficult: the illness that had invaded me and made me loathe my body was filling me with a paralyzing terror of death. I was not religious. The few times that I surprised myself thinking about God, I was amazed to discover that I felt no concern about the fact that the notion of a vengeful, disciplinarian God, created in man's image in order to give meaning to his life, the God of religion, had no meaning for me. But I was afraid, as I am now, and perhaps always have been: I would have liked to die convinced that after this life the mystery will be revealed.

When I was fifteen, I read somewhere in a book by Koestler that if a man with supernatural strength were able to shoot a magical arrow into infinite space, the arrow would travel beyond the Earth's gravity, beyond the moon, beyond the interstellar forces, and then it would travel past other suns, other galaxies, would cross the Milky Way, the Honeyed Way, and the Acid Way, and would leave behind these nebulous spirals and fly toward other galaxies. There was nothing to stop its course, no limit and no end, and it would continue its endless voyage through time and space. A voyage so cosmic that our poor human brains cannot comprehend it.

The idea of that arrow stayed with me, and some nights I would go out into the garden and stare at the sky and wonder where the soul resided after that long voyage through an immensity without memory or time.

Now I saw myself as that arrow, and the idea frightened me. I was terrified by the notion that this voyage was possible and that I would soon undertake it, and would disappear from my own memory and the memories of others. . . . Clemente would forget me, Aunt Luisa would forget me, Amanda would forget me, and I would lose contact with them so profoundly and so irrevocably that it would be as if I had never existed. I was doomed, there was no doubt about it, this desert before me was the only reality; I could count on nothing else. I had reached the end of the line. One more step, and I would enter the mystery of death.

In any case, I sank completely into these thoughts, the darkest I ever remember having; I saw myself in a dark tunnel with many twists and turns that kept me from seeing the light at the end. My illness passed through that tunnel, my mother's early death passed through the tunnel, Clemente and our marriage passed through the tunnel. . . . Marriage is the most difficult state in which to live with another person. It destroys the enigmas of the relationship between two people, it joins together that which perhaps should never have been joined, things are shared that perhaps should never be shared. Subtly, the partners begin to fall into silence because words begin to lose their luster; that which once seemed like an original idea begins to feel like an idea that has been repeated a million times, dull, tiresome. Over the years, people stop really seeing each other; they no longer rub each other the wrong way, but neither do they provoke passion or fury, there is no reason to make peace. There are no more good-byes at the door, departures at dawn, furtive kisses on the stairs, or dreamy nocturnal wonderings. From marriage forward, kisses become more familiar and less wet, and what comes after the nighttime is more of the same; mad, romantic, magical love comes to an end, and a routine of toilet paper and bills begins. You make love—the horror!—while thinking about the next day's shopping list because your husband doesn't eat this, and that other thing hurts his stomach. . . . I felt a kind of panic as I thought about these calamities that I had experienced in my own marriage, which was no different from so many others.

Clemente Balmaceda was measured and precise, a conscientious and methodical architect with little imagination or vision, a collector of antiques, an expert in art who had no artistic talent of his own, a predictable, gentle man; he treated me with great affection, it is true, but he was boring. In other words, Clemente was what one would call a "good man." Even so—and I say this with something approaching solemnity—after twenty-five years of living together, after tedious days in which I could barely tolerate the monotony of our routine, with one day exactly the same as the next, with everything that life with Clemente signified, Clemente—defects and all, including his six-year affair with Eliana—was irreplaceable, immutable. He had always been so, and would be until the end of my days. I would never stop enjoying the feeling of his feet when I climbed into bed. I had fallen out of love with him long ago. I don't know if I was ever truly in love with him, but this is secondary. There is always one person in a relationship who forces the other to love him. In our case, even though I was the one who had kissed Clemente on the lips, a week after we met at Amanda's house, he was the one who had obliged me to love him. I had taken the first step on a path that he had then compelled me to follow without realizing that I had the choice to turn back. And there were moments when I did love him. At that time in my life I needed a firm base to stand on, a family, a normal life, to live with a person who understood—like most people in the world —that the nighttime is a time to sleep. . . . I loved my father deeply, but my father did not know how to be a family and my home (his home) was in a permanent state of chaos. There was singing in our house; my father played his guitar and crooned the latest romantic ditty he had composed for one of his lady friends, or recited "I Dreamt I Dwelt in Marble Halls," an aria from his favorite opera. We told ghost stories into the wee hours—he had a passion for them—and discussed the results of the horse races. My father would enter a state of mystical exaltation whenever Rosa of Luxembourg won a race. There were always people coming and going, his friends and pretty women whom he invited over almost every day. They played charades, stripping games, and poker on Sundays. But no one bothered about whether the electricity bill had been paid or whether the grass was cut, or if there was bread in the kitchen.

Sometimes loving a person isn't the most important thing, but rather the serenity that person produces in your soul. The truth was that I would not have known how to live if Clemente hadn't existed. My life would have been scattered to the winds. . . . Many times I suspected he must realize that passion was not the motivator in my case, and in a way this thought calmed me, soothed my conscience. In a marriage one can simulate almost anything, but lack of passion is revealed by the eyes, in the pupils, in the tone of voice, in the way one moves. It is apparent in every gesture, in everything we say and do. . . . Clemente must have glimpsed it in my movements, in my silences.

A few years ago we traveled to London and stayed at the Plaza Hotel, across from Hyde Park. We took a walk one morning. We went along one side of the park toward Oxford Street, then continued to Bond Street, down Old Bond Street and Regent Street to Picadilly Circus. I was thinking about an article by Valentine Low that I had read the previous day in the *Evening Standard*, a meditation on the complex relationship between the English and Americans ("The United States is a foreign country; we will never understand each other") and at that moment a double-decker bus almost ran us over (the damned traffic on the wrong side of the street). Clemente pressed me against his body and we stood like that for a few moments. Now that I think of it, we must have looked quite ridiculous embracing in the middle of the street. If someone saw us, he would have thought we had chosen a strange time to patch things up. When we finally reached the sidewalk, Clemente took my hand and asked me: "Do you love me?" I didn't know what to say. He had caught me off guard. "Of course I do," I answered, and he looked at me with a touch of sadness. We took the underground to Embankment and visited the Houses of Parliament. "Please remove your hat, sir, you are in the palace of government," a guard said to Clemente. That day he had decided to wear a jockey cap from Harrod's, in the style of the Duke of Windsor. We visited the Palace, "the fart factory," as the boatman who took us down the Thames to the Tower of London later that morning called it. At around noon we went to the Red Lion pub in Whitehall and ordered fish and chips. "I'm so glad," Clemente said out of the blue and apropos of nothing. When I asked him what he meant, he answered: "I'm so glad you love me." In other words, he had been thinking about what I had said during the three hours between the time we had embraced in the middle of the street and that moment. I was silent; what could I say? But it stayed with me and I have asked myself many times whether one should remain bound to a man whom one does not love passionately.

I have always envied the strength that allowed my father to survive my mother's problems and to live his life despite her depression and premature death. I reproached him for his irresponsibility and lack of good sense, but couldn't help but admire his grip on life, his disdain for any kind of formality, and his youthfulness, despite each passing birthday. These were all qualities that

43

would have suited a character in a novel, but they were disastrous in the guardian of a frightened, insecure child. When I decided to go out with Clemente, after our conversation in Amanda's garden, I was choosing security. That well-mannered, respectful young man who was about to receive his architectural degree was the exact opposite of everything I had experienced in my father's house. I wanted to live in an "appropriate" manner, and the appropriate thing was to have a normal family, a dining room where the mother, father, and children sit together at the table, an orderly house, a schedule that takes into consideration the schedules of all the other members of the family. My father dined at midnight because he did not like to sleep. He liked to say: "I'll have all the time in the world to sleep after I'm dead."

Afterward, looking back from the orderly routine of my married life, I missed that life, how he used to sit on a chair by the fireplace, telling stories until three in the morning, his profile silhouetted against the flames; the lies he used to tell his creditors; his pointy chin; his thick cheeks; his huge, bony, beak-like nose, which fascinated me as a child, as if it had a music all its own. I felt nostalgia for a particular evening he had come home drunker than usual and told me that he had fallen in love with a writer twenty years his senior, and that he wanted me to meet her. "She's bewitching, cultivated, intelligent, a goddess of love and of literature. The only problem is she's a feminist," he gushed, the cotton-wool in his mouth in no way dampening his enthusiasm. I found it hard to believe that he had fallen for a woman so much older than he was—he usually ran after young, beautiful girls, no matter how silly they were—and it seemed even more unlikely that a feminist could have fallen for such a mess of a man, but my father's affairs always had a touch of unsuitability and contradiction. . . . I can barely remember his face toward the end of his life. His features have slowly eroded from my memory, despite my efforts to retain them. The face that looks out at me from the photograph on my chest of drawers, taken when he was sixty, is practically that of a stranger. In those last days, his face was different, and that face—of which I have no photographs—has disappeared. But I will always remember his fragrance: a mix of tango, strong cologne, and expensive hair cream.

Fleeing the insecurity this man inspired in me, and wrapped in my own contradictions, I chose the firm ground of marriage and came to Clemente with a mixture of expectation and illusions, which lasted a few years and then began to dissolve. Eventually, my feelings for him became something that to this day I don't know exactly how to define. All I know is that Clemente is the only person in this world in whose presence I am not ashamed to die.

{The Notebook}

It was a warm, clear midsummer night. The city of Santiago was empty. In the house, as always, there were no loud noises, nothing moved, there were no raised voices or peals of laughter. "Clara is right, it is an empty place, slowly filling up with unhappiness," Clemente thought to himself.

Clara was asleep. She seemed to be dreaming. Her lips moved as if she were praying and her eyes darted back and forth behind her eyelids. From time to time she shook her hands as if swatting away flies.

Clemente sat and watched her for a long time, and then went down to read the notebook. He had made a small mark on the page where he had stopped the other night.

". . . and then it would travel past other suns, other

galaxies, would cross the Milky Way, the Honeyed Way, and the Acid Way, and would leave behind these nebulous spirals and fly toward other galaxies. There was nothing to stop its course, no limit and no end, and it would continue its endless voyage through time and space. . . ."

How often, walking down a street or driving to Viña del Mar, these words had returned to his memory. Clara had read this passage in a book by Arthur Koestler and then read it out loud to him. It was on a night when they stopped in Constitución, near Molco. He had never struggled with the idea of death, or had any relationship at all with death; it was a subject he always tried to avoid because it made him terribly tense. But the idea of a magical arrow traveling through the immensity of space had affected him deeply. He did not like to think about it—he did not particularly like to lose himself in existential questions—but yes, it was enough to drive you mad if you started to think about what happens next, and where do we all go? As a child he had tormented himself with the thought that reality was actually a figment of his imagination, that the name Clemente existed only in his mind, that nothing was real. . . . As an adult, he had shut the door on all these metaphysical doubts.

He pushed the notebook away and thought back to their trip to Molco, or what was left of Molco, the ashes of Molco. "My childhood tomb," as Clara had called it. It was the only time they had gone there together and the first time Clara had returned since the estate had been expropriated in 1968. The rambling old house had been abandoned since then and was a dilapidated ruin. The walls were peeling, the floorboards were cracked, some of the beams had fallen down, many of the roof tiles were gone, and there were bushes and weeds growing everywhere, peeking out of the floors. There was dog excrement in the rooms. A Spanish hen—the only one left in that world of pine trees and paths cut through the rich earth—scratched around the patio with the hortensias. This is where my grandmother slept, this was the children's room; you see that hill? Enedina lived there. . . . Clara recreated the world of her childhood for him, her eyes shimmering with emotion. A part of her had been buried in that land where she had lived until just after her mother's suicide. It was buried deeply, and she almost never spoke of those times. Some day I'll write it all down, she would say, but she never did. Well, now she was finally doing it, Clemente thought, sighing as he looked down at the notebook.

That day they had spent the whole afternoon wandering around the property as Clara recovered the sounds and smells from her past, and searched for the shade of the eucalyptus trees that the subsequent owners had cut down for wood and the grazing fields that had disappeared beneath an invasion of pines. When they arrived she insisted they climb to the top of the Luciérnagas hill. She wanted to look over the place that she had thought about for so many years. "All these years I dreamed about this road down to the threshing floor, the clearing in the forest and the cypress tree where Enedina hung herself, the ravine, and to the right, Adela's house, and beyond that the marsh and the summit of Mount Trauco, and even farther away, the grayish ridge that goes on and on forever."

Clemente listened to her, overcome. He had no idea this place was so important to her, or that she remembered it in such detail. . . . There were too many things about Clara that he knew nothing about.

When they reached the top of the hill and Clara searched the entire length of the landscape she let out a gasp.

"It's not as I remember it," she said, holding her hand up to her forehead like a visor. "I can't see the marsh, or the threshing floor or the fences that marked the boundary of San Alfonso, or the vineyards that used to grow on one of the slopes of the Trauco. Gilberto's house isn't there anymore, nor is the path that led to the Toribia estuary. Even the estuary has disappeared."

She sounded disconsolate.

"They've filled it with pines," she declared. They went back down to the house.

"This is where Enedina lived," she said when they passed a place where one could see nothing but pines. "Her house was right here."

"Who was Enedina?" Clemente asked, intrigued, and she told him that Enedina was a pale, distracted, woman who almost never spoke. She had hung herself one night from the branch of a cypress tree in the eucalyptus forest. She said nothing more and he did not ask any questions out of fear of stirring up memories of her mother.

That trip had taken place in 1978, fifteen years ago, but perhaps the idea of the arrow had stayed in her heart and mind all those years. She was always so reserved. So quiet. So uncommunicative. He looked mistrustfully at the notebook, as if it were an enemy, and then put it back in the drawer.

Clara would have been a good writer; she had the imagination for it, but made up for it with a lack of discipline. She was a dilettante. She had talent for everything she did, but she never pushed her talent into any concrete action. She was a voracious reader. Clemente would watch out of the corner of his eye as she took notes in a notebook while she read. She read like an academic, sitting at a table, pencil in hand and notebook at her side.

"What are you writing?"

"Just words I don't know."

One day she showed him the things she had written when she was a little girl, in Molco. Clemente was amazed; they were wonderful stories, filled with magic and poetry. There was one in particular he loved. It was about an old lady without teeth who took a bath in a tub of water mixed with her own urine to arouse her husband. And there was another one about a grandfather who went senile and wandered at night with his cane looking for lambs; when he found one, he would beat it to death with the cane. . . .

It was one o'clock in the morning and a branch of the walnut tree tapped the window lightly. Outside lay the rest of the world: couples returning from parties, teasing one another in the street; cars stopped at red lights; elderly men and women asleep in their beds; busy bars filled with people talking loudly; street urchins sniffing glue under bridges; dogs digging through overturned garbage cans; flies; prostitutes waiting on corners. And there they were, the two of them, on this side. Damn Clara's illness, damn the uncertainty and the not knowing what the hell it all meant, damn the destiny of man, condemned to the company of worms who will be the only ones to attest to the marvel of the brain and eyes.

He turned out the light and stayed there, sitting in front of the window, his gaze wandering through the darkness.

A STRANGER IN A CAFÉ

A woman walked by and peered at me curiously, as if she had seen me before but couldn't quite remember where. It looked as if she might stop and say hello, but then she kept walking, smiling slightly as if to apologize for what she probably took to be a mistake on her part. She moved like someone much younger than her age. She was on the heavy side, but very well preserved. She had probably recently lost her husband; she was dressed in black, like a widow. There was not the slightest touch of color in her attire, except for her attractive blood-red lipstick. "She must be twenty-five years older than I am," I thought, and wondered what her life had been like twenty-five years earlier. Perhaps she had experienced a dilemma like the one I was living through now. . . . But the woman did not look like someone who had spent the previous decades living the routine of a worn-out marriage, and even less like someone suffering from a serious illness. She looked too healthy, too erect, proud, and relaxed in her way of moving; I did not think she had spent the last few years with a husband whom she simultaneously needed and was tired of. I was convinced that she had been happy in life and that her name was Pilar. Of course, lately, my ability to guess people's names had been failing to an alarming degree. Ever since I was a child, I have had the strange habit of naming the people I see in the street, their children, their wives, their husbands. It began as a game I played with Amanda: "His name must be Juan, that man's wife must be called Alicia, I bet that guy's name is Ernesto." We would place bets, doubled over laughing at our antics, and sometimes we would even have the courage to go up and ask the person what his name was. Over the years, Amanda had given up the game and packed it away with her childhood amusements; for me, it became an obsession that has stayed with me to this day. Whenever I'm on the bus I peer into people's faces, study their gestures, consider the size and shape of their earlobes; I take into account whether they are fat or tall, I look at their eyebrows, their jaw, and whether it closes evenly or is misaligned because of the placement of the molars. I check the color of their teeth, and whether their nose hairs are visible, and the depth of the furrow of their brow. Suddenly a light goes off in my mind and the name comes to me: her name is Adela. On several occasions, as an adult, I have had the gumption to ask the person her name, and sometimes I got it right. I was convinced I had special powers. But lately my powers have been vastly diminished; perhaps the illness is clouding my telepathic field of vision. One day while I was waiting at a bus stop, I got up the courage to ask a lame, toothless dwarf whether his name was Gilberto. The man tilted his oversized head up at me and, fixing me with a cold look of hatred, hissed: "Bitch!" I walked away from the bus stop as quickly as my legs would carry me, feeling abused, and became convinced that the man's name was actually Arturo. God knows who this Gilberto was, who had caused such anger in him; perhaps he had stolen his wife. . . . But this time I felt sure; the woman's name was Pilar.

I kept watching her. She was walking toward Calle Tobalaba. She was probably going to the beauty parlor on the corner. She looked like a grandmother who has her hair done every Saturday morning, then goes to her daughter's house for lunch with her grandchildren and in the afternoon plays canasta with three childhood friends. Between one game and the next, they drink watered-down whiskey and consume shrimp and asparagus canapés: ("Oh dear, I'm gaining weight. A woman who has just lost her husband should not have such an appetite.")

At the corner, the woman had entered the shop next to the bakery. So I was right, she was going to get her hair done. Her face stayed with me. I remember it perfectly. Her eyes and plump lips were still youthful. She must have been beautiful; she probably had a fascinating life with a man who knew how to make her laugh. A person's face is the mirror of her soul, but also the mirror of her partner in life; when that person is gone, it becomes the reflection of the dearly departed.

I got up, feeling that the lady had somehow cleared my mind and helped me to emerge from my dark tunnel. "If I survive and in twenty-five years I can carry myself like that," I thought, "with a regal air and a halo of satisfaction for a life well lived, then it means that today's torment was worth it."

My mood suddenly improved. "Enough! I'm drowning in a puddle, repeating the boring litany muttered by every traditional wife in this world. I sound like those rich ladies with too much time on their hands and nothing to do with their lives but torture the help and resent their husbands." I drove away the dark thoughts that had been tormenting me since my vision of the old lady and started walking again, feeling much better.

"An espresso, please," I said to the waiter at a café where I had stopped to rest for a moment. I had walked about fifteen blocks and a cup of coffee—and the glass of mineral water that came with it—were just what I needed. The place was almost empty. It was still early. The shops on Calle Providencia were starting to open. At the next table there was a lady with a child of about ten who was drinking a Coke, and in the corner, next to the window, a man. He caught my attention because he looked like Clemente when he was young. He could have been in his fifties, and was slender and attractive. He had a long face with angular cheekbones, a high fore-head, dense eyebrows, and the same gawky appearance that Clemente had when he was twenty. He was wear-ing dark blue corduroy trousers and a nice gray sweater with a pattern of yellow, gray, and blue rhombuses. His white shirt illuminated his somewhat gaunt features. As I raised the cup to my lips, our eyes met. I turned away and began to mentally go through the list of ingredi-ents that Clemente had requested for his sauce. He had left very early for Viña del Mar to supervise the con-struction site. He would be away all day, but would return before eight to prepare the sauce. "He will be on time, as usual," I thought, hurrying to finish my coffee. Clemente was never late. He possessed an exasperating sense of punctuality. His life functioned like a Swiss watch, but one hour ahead of everyone else; when it was four o'clock for the rest of the world, it was already five o'clock for him. Every day he did the same things at the same time. Clemente did not possess even a hint of the messiness that is typical of architects. His routine was invariable: he woke up at six thirty, drank some water from a glass he had placed on his nightstand the night before, stepped into the bathroom with his radio— a small portable radio that kept him company while he took his shower—and argued out loud with the morning newscast. He listened to the same station every morning. "Why do you argue? He can't hear you!" I would ask him from the bedroom, but he couldn't hear me over the noise of the shower. A little while later he would emerge from the bathroom, wrapped in his white towel, and dress in silence. Then he would sit at the black Florentine marble table by the window and read the paper, taking slow sips from the cup of *café con leche* that Justina had left for him. Finally, he would come over to the bed where I lay awake or half-awake, kiss me on the forehead, and go off to work.

The man in the café looked at me again and smiled. There was something slightly melancholy about his smile; it was a nice smile, a frank smile. I picked up my coffee cup and pretended to take a sip. I remember I noticed his long fingers and his hairy arms. I could see the dark hair peeking out of the neck of his sweater and on his wrist, around his flat, square watch. I crossed and uncrossed my legs and turned toward the counter. He continued to watch me. I could feel his eyes on my profile. I stayed like that for a moment, avoiding his gaze as he sought out mine. I started to feel uncomfortable with those eyes watching me, seemingly planted on my face forever.

The whole time we sat in the café—as I avoided his persistent gaze and he insistently tried to get me to turn my head—I felt sure that this stranger was not one of those men who go around wearing their male hormones on their sleeves, undressing with their eyes every woman who crosses their path. There was something about him that was profoundly different from the bovine, libidinous stare of those men, who mentally remove your undergarments and invade the darkest reaches of your intimacy.

"Please bring me another coffee," I asked the waiter. "First you have to pay at the register, *Señora*." I'm not sure why it bothered me that he had called me *Señora*. At that point the stranger reached into his pocket, took out a few coins and dropped them on the table, got up, and walked out.

I also left the café a few minutes later. I stopped at the window of a bookstore in the same passageway where the café was, not to look at a book, but to check my reflection. I wanted to see how that man—who had so resembled the young Clemente—had seen me. I wanted to judge whether I looked older or younger than my age, to see if I was still pretty. Most of all, I wanted to see if death was peeking out of the corner of my eyes, if the illness that had altered my soul had also affected my face. Had he seen me, or just my shadow? "I'll pretend that I'm someone who has just seen me in the street," I thought as I looked at my reflection. What I saw there, and what hit me like a bolt of lightning, was the back of the man from the café. He was standing in front of a housewares shop, probably looking at my reflection in the glass, just as I was looking at his. We stood there for a long time, pretending to scan our respective shop windows. What could he be looking for in the display window of a houseware store? Perhaps he was thinking of buying a present for his wife. Or perhaps the object he was looking for was not for his wife but for his lover. And why did it have to be a gift for someone else? Perhaps he lived alone. Maybe he was a bachelor. Or a widower. Yes, a widower. He didn't look like a bachelor, I thought. His wife's name was probably Elena. He must be newly widowed. I bet his name is Pedro. Men with that name have a mystical, ungainly look. . . . Perhaps he recently moved to a small apartment and is beginning a new chapter in his life. He must feel lost, poor thing, walking around Providencia street on a Saturday morning, early enough to make one think that he spent the night alone. He's just killing time, waiting for something, looking at some coffee cups. . . .

After a while I stopped formulating ridiculous conjectures and theories and decided to continue walking toward the market. It was difficult to take my leave of the stranger (or rather of the stranger's back). As I passed by him, he did not move. He probably did not want to look directly into my face, but I was sure he had seen my reflection in the window and was waiting for me to leave before leaving himself. I almost thought I caught some slight change in his face, a quick expression, like a smile.

On the next block there is an old mansion that once belonged to Amanda's parents. This is where, many years ago, I met Clemente, on a December afternoon beneath one of those clear blue skies that we used to have in Santiago. The house was now an embassy. As I passed the wrought iron gates—the same wrought iron gates—I remembered that afternoon and felt as though I had almost caught a whiff of the rose bushes Amanda's mother used to cultivate and care for as if they were her children. I looked up at the windows on the second floor and felt the nostalgia that invades us when we think back to a time so distant that it feels like a dream. I remembered the lunches beneath those same trees, and Amanda's mother walking around the garden in her white hat, shears in her gloved hand, exclaiming at the perfection of her roses. "I envy you, Amanda; you don't know what I would have given for a mother who was truly involved in life and who wasn't dying of anything."

I looked at the centuries-old chestnuts and heard my own voice calling out from somewhere by the pool in the corner of the huge garden. One day when Amanda and I were there alone, and I was about to jump into the pool without my bathing suit, a stranger had climbed out from behind the bushes and startled me.

"Now that you've seen me naked, you'll have to marry me," I said, covering myself precipitously with a towel.

He looked me up and down, as if my body were still uncovered, and nodded.

"I accept."

I dressed behind some bushes and returned to the spot where he was still waiting for me.

"Let me introduce myself. I'm Clemente Balmaceda," he said, holding out his hand.

"Clara, Clara Griffin," I answered.

We sat on two wicker chairs on the lawn and started a lengthy conversation. He was in class with Amanda's brother. He had come by on the wrong day. Javier had invited him to swim on the next day. But thanks to his lucky mistake, he had had the opportunity to see a pretty girl in the nude. He was sweet and charming. He smelled clean, like freshly sliced lemon, and his ungainliness pleased me as much as the way he looked at me. In those days, I was full of complexes; I felt ugly and skinny, and I thought I looked like a prematurely old woman. I had a strong desire to please. He told me he was in his last year of architecture school. He told me about his plans. He dreamed of becoming an urban planner and doing something to make sense of this chaotic city. I told him about my father, who was the center of my existence. . . . I talked for a long time about this fun-loving, pleasure-seeking man who would come home at any time of day or night calling out "Here I am." This was completely unnecessary, of course; if there was one person in this world who didn't need to be announced it was he. He was always, if not drunk, then at least slightly tipsy.

"Is he an alcoholic?" Clemente had asked me.

I explained that like any self-respecting descendant of Irishmen he was a drinker, but that he was never violent or aggressive, or disheveled or unkempt. He never neglected his attire. To the contrary. He gave off a whiff of expensive cologne that mixed well with the scent of his Ducado cigarettes, which he had been smoking from as far back as I could remember and which he imported from Spain. My father spent more time obtaining those smelly cigarettes than he did at any job. His camel hair coat went everywhere with him and there was not a day when he didn't dress himself with great care and put on a fine Italian silk tie, as if he had an appointment with a beautiful woman. He was in love with life. "Cicadas are meant to die singing," he liked to say. He did not die singing, but rather reading *Dubliners*—the only legacy of his romance with the writer twenty years his senior. He died just before his eighty-fifth birthday, and his eyes never lost their twinkle or expressed the slightest fear. His voice never broke, nor did he give off that fatigued air so often present in older people. My father was a pain in the neck, but I loved him despite all the binges and the drinking. I respected him and he made me laugh, but at the same time I hated the fact that he could never pay the bills, and his excessive informality, his perennial disorder. I never blamed my mother's illness or death on the way he lived his life, but at the same time, I realized it could not have been easy to be married to that silly man.

We talked until six in the afternoon. Clemente told me about his valiant, widowed mother, whose gloomy outlook had marked his childhood. Before saying goodbye, I found the courage to tell him about my first sexual experience with Samuel, my boyfriend when I was sixteen. It happened on a hot afternoon in November. We had planned our trip for weeks and talked about it in secret, like two hungry thieves preparing to steal a chocolate cake. It would help us "get to know each other better," he said. I was a virgin and I was so excited by the idea of peeking into the mysterious world of sex that I did not eat for two days. At the time, Samuel was a scrawny kid, covered with pimples, and I was halfway between the pudginess of puberty and my next growth spurt.

We got off of our bikes, practically running, and began to embrace and roll around on the grass. I had so little clue of what was going on that I was not even clear about what would happen next. Each movement seemed like a step toward the revelation of a great mystery, and I was there to give in to whatever was asked of me. It was like something out of one of those Corín Tellado romance novels Amanda and I had read together— except there was nothing soft or silky about it, despite what the Spanish author said. Samuel rubbed up against my body with a kind of rage and after some desperate struggling he began to stammer disconnected words. I thought I heard him let out a sob, but I wasn't sure. In any case it did not take long to figure out what was happening. The genetic memory passed down from great-grandmothers to grandmothers and from mothers to daughters told me something had gone wrong. The rest I could read on Samuel's face.

"It doesn't matter. We'll try again some other time," I said.

"Of course it matters," Samuel murmured, pale and trembling.

We headed home like two defeated warriors, heads hanging, silent, pedaling methodically, our eyes on the front wheels of our bicycles. At the door, as we said good-bye, I repeated that it didn't matter, but Samuel said nothing. . . . I never saw him again. I owe my passion for books to him. In order to forget our catastrophic attempt and overcome my fear of never being able to please a man, I became an avid reader. I slept less and less and read more and more. I could dream that none of this had ever happened and put myself in the place of the heroine of whatever book I was reading. As the powerful thrall washed over me, the memory of Samuel receded farther and farther.

Clemente listened to my story carefully, without comment. I don't think he found it funny. I regretted having told it to him. . . .

We were married one year later, and now, standing in front of Amanda's old house, I saw myself again as I entered the Vitacura church on the arm of my father, who descended the nave fully aware of the solemnity of the moment. His eyes were a lake of tears, caused by emotion and nerves. He had not touched a drop of whiskey for two weeks. "I want to be sober and fresh on your wedding day, like a rose, even if I wilt," he would say as he slurped his lemonade. I still have my white taffeta dress, embroidered with pearls, in a trunk in the attic. Some nights I can still feel the pressure of his hand on my elbow as he led me to the prie-dieu in front of the altar.

{The Notebook}

The Viennese clock struck three in the morning in its deep tones that reminded him of a chime in an abandoned convent, and Clemente sensed his own internal silence. He closed the notebook and began to cry.

Clara's words climbed up the walls of his brain like poisonous spiders. The discovery that Clara knew she was going to die and was suffering aggravated the sense of powerlessness that had filled him since that fateful night when Clara emerged from the bathroom pale and trembling and said: "My nipple is bleeding." But nothing tormented him as much as the discovery that Clara did not know if she had ever loved him and believed she had never been happy with him. What were these serpentine hisses, these waves of arch indifference, this absence of love, supposed to mean? What the devil was

this notebook he was reading? A testament, a long letter addressed to him, a confession before dying? How
was it possible that Clara knew about his affair with
Eliana and yet said nothing, had never made a scene,
screamed, insulted him, slammed the door? Was it indifference or pride? Suddenly he felt profoundly betrayed, like a stupid adolescent humiliated by an older
woman. Clara had been deceiving him all these years
in the worst possible way; she had lied in her attitude
toward him. Their marriage was not, as he had always
believed it to be, an open space in which every feeling
occupied its proper place, just as Clara saw their house,
in which she now claimed she had never been happy.
Instead, it turned out that it was a chaotic tundra. Clara
had tricked him into thinking that things were going
well and that she loved him. . . . Or perhaps that wasn't
quite right. Perhaps he was the one who had not wanted
to recognize the wall between them, Clara's sideways
glances when they sat at the dining table, the way she
looked away when she felt him looking at her, the
manner in which she suddenly changed the subject and
pretended to forget something urgent she needed to tell
him. Perhaps he was the one who refused to admit that
he was profoundly disturbed by his wife's fierce control over her emotions, that formal, tense air she always

had, the way she held herself in check and appeared almost perfect, elegant at all times and under all circumstances, even at the hour of her death. Suddenly he felt that he was standing before the great mystery of Clara, the impossibility of really knowing her, of understanding who she really was. Perhaps there was another Clara, a hidden Clara, or more precisely a Clara that had been hidden from him. This notebook was a clue. It seemed to have been written by another person. That story about Samuel was an example; Clara had never told him that story. He remembered their first conversation next to Amanda's pool very clearly, as well as Clara's beautiful body, which he had glimpsed for only a few seconds, but this story about the bicycle escapade. . . . Clara had never mentioned a first love, except for the young *mirista*[2] she met during a night out on the town with Amanda. He couldn't understand why she would want to invent this grotesque episode which, on top of everything else, seemed so unlikely for a sixteen-year-old, practically a child. . . . He didn't recognize Clara in this story. She was tidy and rather on the distant side; she always seemed to be far away from her interlocutor, as

---

[2] Name given to the members of MIR, the *Movimiento de Izquierda Revolucionaria* (Movement of the Revolutionary Left), many of whom were killed or tortured by the Pinochet regime.

if there were a glass wall between her and the rest of the world. Her trademarks were prudence, caution, moderation. The only time she seemed to lose her common sense was when she indulged her obsession with approaching people on the street and asking their names. Apart from that, Clemente had never seen a more judicious person. The hand that was writing these words was that of a much more sensual woman, a woman with a taste for sex. . . . The Clara who had shared his bed all those years was on the cold side; she had never seemed very interested in sex. . . . And then there was this lover she had invented and to whom she had the audacity to give the name of a real person. If Alberto's friend, Hyde, ever found out about this diary, testament, letter, or whatever it was, in which his full name appeared and in which he played the role of the author's lover, and then was killed off . . . But Hyde would never see the notebook, because Clemente was determined that this dirty laundry never see the light of day, even if it meant he had to confront Clara, sick as she was.

Trapped between sadness and anger he opened the notebook again and reread a few phrases here and there. There were many references to a lack of affection: "I have asked myself many times whether one should remain bound to a man whom one does not love passionately"; "Clemente Balmaceda," she used the full name for maximum effect, "was measured and precise, a conscientious and methodical architect with little imagination or vision, a collector of antiques, an expert in art who had no artistic talent of his own, a predictable, affectionate man; he treated me with great fondness, it is true, but he was boring. In other words, Clemente was what one would call a 'good man.'" A loser, a naïf with good taste but few ideas, a tiresome fool, a bore, Clemente thought to himself, on the edge of desperation. "I had fallen out of love with him long ago," he read elsewhere. . . . He did not feel passion for her either. Passion was the first thing to go, but passion was not everything in a marriage, it was not even the most important thing. In this he agreed with Clara: all marriages become stale over time, but love, tenderness, those feelings were different. But where was her tenderness toward him? He continued to flip through the text. . . . The story of the man in the café was absurd, like something out of a romance novel for young girls. He found the image of Clara avidly watching the man who looked like a younger version of himself utterly pathetic, as he did the idea that she might take offense at the waiter referring to her as *Señora* or the notion that she would stand in front of a shop window waiting for a man to approach and speak to her. . . . It was pathetic.

There were three or four more chapters left, but he did not have the strength to go on. He placed the notebook back in the drawer.

LIONEL HYDE

When I got home from the market, Justina helped me with the bags and handed me a letter from Amanda. I put it in my pocket to read later, calmly, and I ate an apple. Then I went up to my room. I needed to rest. My bed was the only thing in that house that had been chosen by me, in accordance with my taste. I did not let Clemente impose the horror that he had bought from his antiques dealer in Valparaíso. A bed is a turbulent place in which we meditate, dream, imagine, languish, recover, and reproduce. It is the only place where we allow ourselves to fall into a state of absolute oblivion, like a foretaste of death that removes us from the earth. Our bed is a completely secure place—perhaps the only one—where we can enclose ourselves as if we were in a nest. Clemente had selected, for this purpose—a purpose that takes up almost half of our lives—a ridiculously palatial English nuptial bed with heavy yellow brocade curtains, crowned by a kind of Chinese pagoda, with carved eagles and four dragons hanging from each post. The fourth Duke of Beaufort had it made in 1792 for his house in Badminton, Clemente explained proudly, showing off his new purchase. Only a madwoman would have agreed to sleep in that horrifying sepulcher that the fourth duke or whatever he was had found so absurd that he decided to give it away to his antiques dealer. Because in the third world everything is considered a novelty, and a bed belonging to a duke is worth its weight in gold, the dealer had sent this monstrosity to Valparaíso where there will always be a Clemente Balmaceda, willing to believe any story. I made my position clear, and should tears have been required I would have been prepared to shed them. I would not sleep in that bed. It was stored in the cellar of Clemente's office, waiting for the day I died.

I stretched out on my simple bed made out of pine and bought at the Sur furniture store to read Amanda's letter. Her letters were therapeutic. She had been living in Pennsylvania for the last ten years with her American husband, who adored her and whom she adored. She led an orderly, peaceful life, a life out of a

Hollywood movie. It seemed idyllic to her, and the most boring, dullest life in the world to me. One can only tolerate that kind of life under one of two circumstances: if one is born in a suburb on the East Coast where nothing ever happens, or else if one has been beaten down by life in the third world and its chaos, its murderous dictators, its mediocre salaries, intolerable machismo, buses crowded with poor people, and irreparable plumbing. Such a life is desirable only if this chaotic world has become intolerable and your only choices are suicide or marrying an American because you can't take it anymore. Amanda married an American and went to live in a suburb of Philadelphia, within the white walls of her lovely house in a forest, where she wrote novels and articles, cooked, read Shakespeare, and shooed away the squirrels who dug up her tulip bulbs and nibbled on the young azalea buds. "I don't think it is possible to be happier than I have been here," she wrote, and I found it difficult to believe that someone could make such an assertion in writing. Amanda did not know about my illness, and I did not intend to tell her about it. I did not want to tell anyone and at the time, other than the doctors, Aunt Luisa, Clemente, and Justina, no one knew I was sick. I was inhibited by a mixture of shame and fear that the more people knew about it, the more quickly the illness would spread through my body. And I was horrified, truly horrified, by people's compassion. Under normal circumstances I would have told Amanda, but I decided not to, not because I feared her commiseration, but because she had not yet recovered from the shock of her father's terrible death in a car accident in New York.

I put her letter away with the others and shut my eyes. Then I floated off into one of those slumbers filled with gray skies and warm breezes, in which one floats refreshingly. I felt my body relax. The world regained its order as I floated into infinity, light and soft, weightless, without anguish or fear of drowning. I was no longer sick, I felt well, the tumor was a nightmare and not an actual reality within my body; I was free, completely free, what joy, what rest. . . . The last thing I saw before sinking into unconsciousness was a bird crossing the horizon.

Clemente returned from Viña del Mar just before seven, as we had agreed. He was enthusiastic about his newest purchase. After lunch he had taken advantage of a short break to go see his antiques dealer at the harbor. The dealer had called him over; Clemente was an old customer and he had set aside something special for him. He took him to the storeroom and showed him two

Japanese polychrome porcelain figures, which Clemente was now showing me enthusiastically. "They're exquisite, just look at them!" he said, picking up one of the figures, which was in the shape of two half-naked men locked in a wrestling embrace. "These are extremely rare pieces from 1688, a real find. Artists working in porcelain in the seventeenth century almost never represented the human form. They usually made animals, especially tigers, or vessels, like vases, or plates. These wrestlers are truly unique. The third figure in this group is in Burghley's inventory, in London; that's how we know they are from 1688. What do you think? Aren't they wonderful?"

"Where are you planning to put them?" I asked. Clemente turned his head and pressed his lips together, as he often did when he was reflecting. He pointed to the stone step in front of the fireplace, as if he had always known that this was the exact spot for these porcelain figures, as if he had been looking for years for just these figures to put precisely in that spot.

"Each thing has its place," he said, walking over to the chimney and positioning the two figures on the step across from the marble Buddha.

He was in a very good mood. He set the two figures down near each other, almost touching, so that they appeared to be a single group of four white gladiators bound together in a struggle. They were beautiful and mysterious, and this truly seemed like the perfect spot for them. Clemente took three steps back and observed them for some time. Then he took two steps forward, then back again. He repeated this three more times, until he seemed completely satisfied. Then he went to the kitchen to prepare the sauce. I went upstairs to take my third shower of the day. I hastily removed my clothes and jumped in the shower, with the water pouring down on my hair. Before my illness I used to distractedly examine my breasts for lumps or tender spots that had not been there the month before; my mind wandered from one thought to the next, and sometimes I hummed one of the tunes my father had loved, or watched the water flowing down without thinking anything at all. After the diagnosis I began to shower hesitantly, like a blind person. This time, I let my mind be carried away by the soft, languid feeling of hot water on cold skin. After five minutes under the comforting jet I felt myself crying torrents of tears, disconsolately, as if a flood-gate had opened. And as absurd as it may seem, instead of asking myself why I was crying like this, I began to wash my face with cold water to hide the traces of tears. I could not greet Clemente's friends looking upset.

Now I wonder what would have happened if I had come down to dinner with my eyes swollen and a red face. Perhaps the fibers of this tapestry I am weaving would have formed a different pattern. Clemente's friends would have asked me what was wrong, is something the matter, are you not feeling well? Clemente would have looked at me searchingly, his eyes filled with concern. I would have apologized and said it was nothing, that I wasn't feeling well and just wanted to say hello before retiring to bed, encouraged by our guests and by Clemente. Clemente would have come up later to ask what was wrong, why I had been crying, and he would have caressed my chin and cheeks, and after kissing me on the forehead—a new habit since the diagnosis—he would have shut the door carefully so that I could rest without being disturbed by the noise from downstairs. ("Tomorrow you'll feel better; just try to get some sleep.") But of course at that moment I did not think about this scenario, which has only come to me now that my lover faces eternity in an unknown necropolis, with no memory of me, or of his wife, or of what took place in Almarza's apartment. . . .

When I got out of the shower, I dampened a corner of my towel with cold water and dabbed my eyes. I stood with the towel over my eyes until I could see that the swelling had gone. I pulled my black dress out of the closet, and then I thought to myself: "No, it's a little early yet for a black dress," and smiled at my own dark humor.

At nine o'clock the bell rang and I went downstairs.

"That must be Lionel Hyde. He mentioned he might come early. He just got in from Punta Arenas," Clemente said as he went to answer the door.

I was halfway down the stairs when I heard Clemente greet his guest. Then I heard the guest's voice; it was gravelly and seemed on the verge of cracking. It was the voice of a heavy smoker, a voice I didn't recognize.

"You're early," I heard Clemente say. "Did you have a good flight?"

"Yes, I got in a little while ago. It was very comfortable, thank you," the voice said.

Then I heard him exclaim over the Sèvres vase on the table.

"Where did you get that beautiful vase?"

Clemente dove in, like a fish in water, telling him the story of the vase. He explained that it was from the first batch of fine porcelains made by Sèvres in 1756, during the reign of Louis XV, when the factory was moved from Vincennes to Sèvres. . . .

I was fixing a lock of my hair that kept dropping

over my eyes. When I looked up, I found myself face to face with our deep-voiced guest.

A strange sensation, like a shiver, ran through my back. The stranger smiled as if he had never seen me before and held out his hand.

"You must be Clara. Alberto has told me so much about you. I'm very pleased to meet you."

He said nothing of our encounter that morning. He did not mention our presence in the café, three tables away from each other. He made no reference to the fact that we had seen each other again in the passageway. It was as if none of this had happened, or as if he had no memory of it. But he had to remember. His eyes revealed to me that he remembered all of this perfectly. But he said nothing. He simply held my hand decidedly longer than usual, squeezing it slightly, but not so slightly that I did not realize this was not a typical handshake. He made me complicit in his silence and his lie. It was not true that he had just landed at Pudahuel airport. That morning he had been kicking around Calle Providencia, alone and bored, with nothing to do, not in Punta Arenas.

"How is Blanca?" Clemente asked.

I see! I thought to myself. *So he's not a recent widower and his wife's name is not Elena.*

I was unable to hide a smile at how off the mark my predictions had been. He smiled back at me. I felt a tremor climb up my spine, and at that moment I realized a bridge had been established between us, a bridge that was invisible to Clemente or anyone else, because to the eyes of the rest of the world there was absolutely nothing that could link me with this stranger who was setting foot in our house for the very first time. I couldn't understand how I had suddenly found myself in this situation with the man who, earlier in the day, had reminded me of Clemente. In fact, now that he had his own name he ceased to bear any resemblance to my husband.

Lionel turned toward Clemente and said: "Blanca is very well. I'd like to call her to let her know I've arrived and everything is in order. Would that be all right?"

"What shamelessness!" I thought to myself, and it must have been written on my face because he fixed me with his eyes, clearly ordering me to stay silent. At least, this was how I understood it. We will talk later, you and I, he seemed to be saying. He would explain it all to me. I, of course, said nothing.

"Hello, Cristina? Darling, I didn't know you'd arrived! You arrived yesterday? How lovely! How is everything? Is Blanca home?"

Now I was sure that not only had he not been in

Punta Arenas that morning, but he had been gone from home a few days. Otherwise, he would have known his daughter was in town.

"Hello, Blanca? Yes, I took the afternoon flight. . . . I went directly to Clemente Balmaceda's house. . . . No, don't worry, I've been feeling fine. . . . Yes, of course, I haven't forgotten. I'll call you tomorrow. Don't wait up. I'll be back very late."

How did he know he would return late? Was he going to stop in "Punta Arenas" before going home?

While Lionel was speaking to his wife in Clemente's study, Clemente had gone to the kitchen to fetch the tray of drinks, and I pretended to arrange the flowers on the table in the vestibule, next to the Sèvres vase. "I wonder what it is that he didn't forget to do?" I thought to myself, straightening the gladiolas. Perhaps Blanca had asked him to bring her something from Punta Arenas. But other than a spider crab, a *pejerrey* fish or some ocean breezes, I couldn't imagine what a person might ask a traveler to bring back from Punta Arenas. Maybe she was not referring to an object, but to some sort of engagement, a dinner the following day, or a condolence visit. He had said, "I've been feeling fine." Was he sick? I asked him this two days later, on October 11, when we had a drink at the bar at the Sheraton Hotel. But I don't want to get ahead of myself. I prefer to proceed slowly, so that I can decipher exactly how events unfolded.

When he finished talking and hung up the phone, he came into the living room. I quickly headed in the same direction. I didn't want him to notice I had been listening to his conversation. Clemente came in with the tray. We sat in front of the fireplace. The two of them sat on the stuffed chairs and I took my place at the end of the sofa. At first there was an insipid exchange of isolated comments, the typical things we say when we are only beginning to get to know one another and have few subjects in common. I felt uncomfortable. At one point I decided to get up to fetch more ice, but then I saw that the little bucket was almost full and I sat back down with my hands on my lap hoping that the other guests would arrive soon.

The mysteries of the mind and of human behavior are indecipherable. Or perhaps I am simply an incongruous and eccentric woman who is struggling with the news of her imminent death. . . . How could I have been crazy enough to agree, the very next day, to meet this man at the bar of the Sheraton Hotel? What was I thinking when I said to him on the phone: "Sure, tomorrow at six at the bar on the first floor"? But I'm getting ahead of myself again. It is important that I recount each step and every detail of what happened between those first timid probings of my relationship with Lionel and the moment that his eyes remained fixed on the white ceiling of the room in Almarza's little apartment.

After a few moments in which no one spoke and an angel flew through the room, Lionel said something that seemed to emerge from the most obscure reaches of his mind, almost from his unconscious, the sort of thing a person might say if he has abruptly awoken from a dream.

"Chance is a strange thing."

Clemente and I looked at each other, surprised by this unexpected assertion.

"I've always been intrigued by things that happen by chance," he went on. "I'm amazed by the consequences of a fortuitous meeting. You walk into a café and you see a beautiful woman, and that same evening you see her again, and the next day you call her and invite her out for a drink, and you end up as lovers. Or you miss a plane because the alarm clock didn't go off and the plane crashes, killing all its passengers. Don't you find it overwhelming that something as insignificant as sleeping through an alarm or stopping for a cup of coffee can change your life forever?"

As he said this he stared directly into my eyes. I felt uncomfortable and deeply moved by his nerve in making such a direct reference, in front of my husband, to our meeting at the café that afternoon. I lowered my eyes. What message was he trying to send me?

"What do you mean?" Clemente asked, distractedly, obviously not following the implications of our guest's bold words.

Lionel changed the subject, as if he had been speaking in a dream. He started talking about the upcoming elections. He explained why he was planning to vote for the Green candidate.

I looked at his eyes, an attractive feature of his face. They were more widely set than usual and slightly bulging, but instead of making him less attractive they rendered his face more interesting and less elongated. If Clemente had been paying attention, he would have percieved the intensity of my gaze. But Clemente did not notice how Lionel and I crossed glances during that meaningless conversation, which was anything but. If he had, he would have mentioned it. Despite Eliana, he was jealous, something I could never understand. One would think that a man who has had a lover for several years would not be so concerned about his wife's flirtations.

I suddenly felt irritated and went to put on some music. As I walked toward the study I could feel Lionel's eyes on my back and even when I was in the study I could still feel them, as if they were boring through the wall. I chose Mozart's Concerto no. 19, and the house was filled with bright music, music that seemed to have been composed in order to illuminate the first day of creation. Mozart's music has always filled my heart with joy, and that night, for a moment, it allowed me to forget that my life was hanging by a thread.

"It's too loud!" Clemente called out from the living room. I turned down the volume, slightly.

When I returned to the living room, Lionel was talking about his latest trip to the United States.

"Do you go often?" I asked, and told him that my best friend, Amanda Sierra, a journalist—perhaps he knew her?—lived there.

"I go quite frequently," Lionel said. "I work for a fruit export company, Santa Elena, and I have to go to Philadelphia for business at least three or four times a year."

"Santa Elena? Isn't that Gustavo Almarza's company?" Clemente asked.

"We're partners and good friends. We grew up together in Cauquenes," Lionel answered.

"Are you talking about the senator?" I asked.

"One and the same," said Clemente. "Do you know him?"

At the time I didn't, and I had no way of knowing that my life and his would soon collide.

Life is a time bomb. At that moment, Almarza's name meant nothing to me. I had seen his face on television and in the papers, I had heard him give a speech at the University of Chile, I knew that he had spent a decade in exile, but that was it. Now, the sound of his name fills me with panic.

The doorbell rang.

"Ah, there are the others," Clemente said, getting up.

I could have stayed in the living room with Lionel, but instead I got up hastily—I was afraid of being alone with him—and followed Clemente to the door to receive the arriving guests. They were Alberto López and the other two partners in Clemente's firm.

From then on I felt as if I were on the sidelines. Alberto said he was getting ready to travel around the world with his wife; they were celebrating their thirtieth anniversary. Then they launched into the subject of the new building in Viña del Mar. Lionel did not look at me once during dinner, but that night, late, when he was getting ready to leave and Clemente had gone off to find his coat, he said—or I think he said, or perhaps I dreamt it or willed it—"I'll call you tomorrow."

{The Notebook}

*G*ershwin's mysterious music filled the study. Clemente was sitting at his drawing table with his head in his hands. He could feel his heart throbbing in both temples. Step by step, Clara had begun to tell an unbelievable story, one that on some level he feared might be true. As hard as it was for him to accept, crazy as it sounded, there was a chance that Clara and that man had become lovers. He shuddered. He hoped it wasn't true. He hoped this was all a product of her imagination. But the description of the dinner was accurate. He had arrived early that afternoon to prepare the cocktail sauce for the shrimp, he remembered that perfectly, and he also remembered that he was the one who opened the door for Hyde, and it was true that Hyde said he had just arrived on the afternoon flight and asked to call his wife. Clemente did not remember whether Hyde had spoken with his daughter, but that was not surprising since, according to Clara's description, he was in the kitchen when Hyde made the call. He also did not remember Hyde's comment about chance, but perhaps it had not caught his attention. From the beginning Hyde seemed to him like a bit of an oddball; it wouldn't surprise him if he had brought up the subject of chance and discussed it in those terms. He flipped back to the previous chapters. The walk in London was also just as she had described it, down to the details of the street names. Before they left Chile, Clemente had said that he would board the plane only if she promised not to stop people in the street and ask their names, but such a request was like asking a watermelon patch to produce oranges. She couldn't help herself, and one day she approached the driver of a double-decker bus and asked him if his wife's name was Victoria. The driver looked at her in confusion and said: "Yes, ma'am, it is; have you met my wife?" The description of their walk was completely accurate. As was the bit about Amanda and her idyllic life in the Pennsylvania woods . . . That night or perhaps the following day, he wasn't quite sure, Clara had shown him Amanda's letter. And yes, he was jealous, and always had been, he had to admit it. . . .

Other parts of the story, however, had no basis in reality. He couldn't understand what these inventions were supposed to mean. Where had she gotten the absurd story about the bed with yellow brocade curtains? What was this about a bed that had once belonged to the fourth Duke of Beaufort? He would never have gotten mixed up in such a purchase, especially considering how picky Clara was about her furniture, the fabric for her curtains. . . . Her insistence on making him out to be an old fart obsessed with antiques seemed incomprehensible and unnecessarily cruel. Clemente liked pretty things and he had bought one or two antiques for the house—once he bought a dresser at auction and another time he picked up a Viennese clock at the Rastro market in Madrid—but he did not know any antique dealers in Valparaíso, nor did he know anything about Sèvres porcelain or about seventeenth-century Japanese figurines, and this was the first time he had even heard of the Burghley inventory. Where did Clara get these crazy notions?

His entire being urged him to go up to the second floor where Clara was sleeping, wake her, and throw this monstrous notebook in her face. To clear up the situation with Clara once and for all. Since he began reading these pages he had lived in a constant state of anxiety. During dinner he scrutinized Clara's face to see if he could uncover anything there, a sign that she knew he was reading the notebook, some indication of the disaffection she claimed had been suffocating her all these years, or some evidence of her secret affair. But apart from the fear that he could see in her eyes ever since the day she found out she was ill, he did not notice anything different about her. Did this mean that his wife was a consummate cynic, a professional deceiver? He had trouble believing it, and yet, how could he explain *A Week in October*? Perhaps it was some kind of testament? Why had she never mentioned it to him?

He felt overwhelmed by doubts and for a moment he had the impulse to go upstairs and talk to her, but then he realized he had to put things in perspective. Clara was getting worse. The doctor had said he would probably have to operate again; this time, he wanted to remove her uterus. This was not the most propitious time to talk to her about the notebook, he thought, suspecting that the moment would never come. Clara was right when she said her illness was like an octopus that increasingly invaded the spiritual and physical space of their relationship. It left no room for anything else.

The previous afternoon Clemente had a long conversation with Ana María Constantinau. They had been lovers many years earlier, and despite the fact that their relationship was over—she had thrown a flowerpot at his head—they were still friends, and some days they would call each other and get together for coffee to catch up. Ana María was impulsive and rather opinionated, but she knew how to listen. "I have a problem I need to talk to you about," Clemente said at the pub on Calle Suecia where they had decided to meet. Clara had begged him not to mention her illness to anyone, it was all she asked of him. The only person he had told was Eliana, not so much because it was difficult for him to keep the secret to himself or because he needed to express his feelings of impotence and grief, but rather because he had decided to stop seeing Eliana while Clara was ill, in other words, while she was still alive. Even further: he had decided to put an end to the relationship. He had told Eliana a week after Clara's operation, eight months ago, and since then they had seen each other only a few times. Ana María was a good friend, and he was sure of her prudence and good sense. She looked at him curiously with her enormous green eyes.

"You know you can talk to me about anything. What's wrong?"

"About three weeks ago I found a notebook belonging to Clara in a drawer in the kitchen. I've been reading it, but she doesn't know."

Ana María looked perplexed.

"You've secretly been reading your wife's private journal?"

"No, it's not a journal, or rather it is and it isn't." At that point he realized he had bungled the story and decided to tell her the whole saga from the beginning, starting with Clara's cancer, how he had found the notebook, and a few of the things that were written there.

"How horrible . . . I'm so sorry . . ." murmured Ana María, swallowing her surprise and the embarrassing shock that comes over people when they do not know how to react to an announcement of such gravity. Then she asked:

"When did they discover the cancer?"

"In June of last year. Eight months ago," Clemente said, counting the months on his fingers. "But in the notebook she writes about having a lover."

"Since when?"

"About four months. She met him in October, at a business dinner at my house. Apparently they became lovers almost immediately. I can't tell you more because that's as far as I've gotten. Do you think it could be true? I mean, do you think a woman who has just had a breast removed would go and find a lover? Despite her illness?"

"That's not important," Ana María said.

"What do you mean it's not important?!"

"What I mean is that it doesn't matter if it's true or not, what matters is how strongly she wishes it were true."

"I don't understand."

"Normally a woman would not start an affair while she is battling cancer, but she may strongly desire it, perhaps more than at any other time in her life, in order to feel complete. Women always feel incomplete. Almost all our secrets have to do with something we feel we lack. Our compulsions are connected to this feeling; even our shopping is compulsive, filled with anxiety. The word 'enough' is a masculine word. For women, nothing is ever enough, there will always be something more we need. A man can go through life with a single coat and two pairs of shoes. A woman can't. She needs another coat and another pair of shoes and three more handbags, and another lipstick and another lover, another friend, another problem, and so on to eternity." She laughed.

"I know, but I don't see the connection between this anxiety and the existence of Clara's lover, or hypothetical lover."

"Forget about the lover. What you have to worry about is what she does with this secret. There are secrets and then there are secrets, things that any woman would guard carefully so as not to cause her husband worry, but this is a different kind of secret. We're talking about a woman who has her breast removed, and chooses that moment to find a lover, or invent one, and lets her husband know. That is what matters; what she is saying to herself first of all, and then what she is trying to say to you, not what she does or doesn't do with another man, if that man exists."

"She is not trying to tell me anything. She doesn't know I'm reading the notebook."

"You don't actually think she doesn't realize you're reading it, do you?"

"Don't you think this could be a real secret, in other words something that she doesn't want me to know?"

"Real secrets are not written down; sometimes they are secrets even from ourselves. I wouldn't want to read a real secret written on a piece of paper, even if I had written it myself. There are things that are truly secret, and then there are secrets that want to become reality.

Do you see the difference? Another thing you must consider is that there is nothing that makes a woman more vulnerable than cancer. But it's not the kind of vulnerability that would make her want to fall in love with the first man who crosses her path, but rather the kind that makes her want to find refuge in her husband's arms, in what she knows, in the things she is sure of, in anything that can protect her from death."

Clemente ran his hand across his moist forehead. The bar was full of people, smoke, laughter, and the clinking of glasses.

"An illness like cancer requires a difficult and exhausting struggle. I don't know anyone, married or single, who would choose such a time to become involved in a love affair. But as I said, the mysteries of the soul are great; perhaps when she discovered her desperate situation she felt that life was escaping through her fingers, or perhaps she felt that there was a great void in her life. . . . The two of you don't have children, and you have not been the most faithful of husbands. Who knows, perhaps she felt that her life with you just wasn't enough, and perhaps this novel is the product of her regret that things did not turn out differently. Very few people are content with their lot in life and a novel is often the reflection of that disillusionment. Does she know about Eliana, for example?"

"She knows."

"How do you know?"

"It's in the notebook."

"But she has never said anything to you?"

"No. If you want to know the truth, that is what frightens me the most, somehow. The fact that we've never had a jealous scene, that she's never made the slightest allusion to my relationship with Eliana, that she has never even asked me where I've been when I come home late at night."

"How long do you think she has known?"

"She doesn't say, but apparently for a long time."

"And you couldn't tell? She never revealed it to you in any way? Did she spy on you? Was there anger in her eyes when she looked at you?"

"No, not at all. She knows the affair has been going on for years, but she has simulated ignorance so completely that it would never have occurred to me that she knew."

"You see?"

"What?"

"It's what I was saying before. All of this is part of a larger secret and you have access only to what she wants you to know. It does seem to me like it would be harder to pretend not to know that your husband is having an affair than it would be to find a lover, even if you have cancer. Your wife is a tough nut to crack, what can I say?" Ana María joked, trying to lighten the conversation.

Clemente decided not to tell her that according to the notebook the lover had died. He preferred to leave it at that. They said their good-byes an hour later, and on his way home he reflected more on the idea of what kind of secret this was. He considered calling Hyde at home. He didn't have his number but it would be easy enough to get it. Alberto, his only link to Hyde, was traveling in Europe with his wife, but he could simply call him and ask for the number. Of course it made more sense to speak directly to Clara about this. But he was no longer thinking rationally. He had long since lost his sense of serenity. . . . And to think that before all this he had felt so sure of himself; he went about his business without asking questions, convinced that a touch of ambiguity was like a sprinkle of salt and pepper to spice up his days. It was a way to convince himself that he was not living a monotonous existence. He had been so satisfied with his passionless but harmonious life; what else could he want after all these years . . . ? To think he had lived so contentedly, and then, poof! The splash of cold water, the earthquake, the wild shake-up that yanked him out of his comfortable existence, leaving him immersed in the present mess. How could he be rational under the circumstances?

He put away the Gershwin record and turned out the light on his drawing table. He did not have the courage to go back upstairs and sleep next to Clara. He lay down on the couch in the study and remained awake until the light of the new day, February 26, began to filter through the blinds.

SUNDAY: LOOKING BACK

*H*e had said, "I'll call you tomorrow." That Sunday I made sure to be at home, in the kitchen, expecting his call. I did not even dare to go out on the terrace, fearing that Justina or Clemente might pick up the phone and Lionel would not have the nerve to ask for me. I made up the excuse that I had been wanting to bake a pineapple cake. That way I could stay in the kitchen, near the phone, for most of the morning.

I would like to tell the story of something that happened to me when I was very young. It is an anecdote without great consequence, but it illustrates my state of mind on that Sunday. The difference is that these events took place when I was eighteen years old, and on this Sunday, the tenth of October, I was forty-six. But what can you do. Perhaps when one is waiting for a phone call from a man who could be the embodiment of one's fantasies, it makes no difference whether one is eighteen or forty-six.

The events I am referring to took place one year before I met Clemente. One Saturday afternoon Amanda and I were at her house, bored, unsure of what to do with ourselves. No one had called us to go out, we had no plans, and in those days—it was the sixties—a woman did not take the initiative. If a man didn't call to ask her out for a drink or to go dancing, or to the movies, she was stuck. Suddenly Amanda had an idea: what if we went to El Murciélago? It was the meeting place of all the usual bohemians: actors, students, young leftists and admirers of Che and of the uplifting oratory of Fidel. No one at El Murciélago found his speeches clichéd or overblown or the least bit boring. El Murciélago was one of the few places in Santiago where it would not be strange to see two women alone. It was located at the end of Calle Carmen and was dark as a wine cellar. "*Perfecto distingo lo negro del blanco,*"[3] Violeta Parra's plaintive voice intoned through the smoky and laughter-filled rooms. Amanda and I entered

---

[3] "I have no trouble seeing the difference between black and white," a line from Parra's song "*Gracias a la Vida.*"

as if we were stealing into a cannibal's secret cave, barely avoiding the corners of tables and people's backs in the semi-darkness as we moved toward a spot in the corner.

We ordered two glasses of wine with orange slices.

A little later, once my eyes had adjusted to the low light, I noticed a pair of eyes, square jaw, muscular neck, developed torso, lustrous hair, and the kind of burning look that makes you quake from your head to your toes, a look that instantly and unequivocally reveals that something is going to happen. His beautiful face seduced me. I fell totally in love in two minutes flat, and so did he. It was what is commonly known as a violent crush. Just like that, straight to the marrow and with complete abandon. The man stood up from his stool—he was sitting at the bar—and walked over to us without ever looking away, like a warrior making his way through a battlefield strewn with the bodies of his friends and enemies, as if we were the only two people left on Earth.

"Are you two alone?" he asked, even though it was perfectly clear that we were. "May I join you?"

He pulled over a chair and sat down before we could say anything.

Amanda disappeared, or rather, she was still there, but in the three hours that followed, neither the stranger—

who now had a name, Luciano—nor I noticed her presence. What followed was a long preamble, an introit, a glimpse of paradise; mumbled words, furtive kisses, a hand that touches the forearm and electrifies the body, a mouth next to the ear whispering something only half understood, the foretaste of a delicious morsel. . . . It was all a preview of what would come later, soon, when we were alone.

"I'll call you tomorrow," he said when we parted at Amanda's iron gate. I flew into the house; I had developed wings, I was on the verge of dissolving completely, I was virtually weightless.

The following day would go down in the history of my early life as one of those unlucky moments when one ping-pongs between the desire to die on the spot and an instant reawakening each time Amanda's phone—which rang mercilessly all day long—ignited my hopes once again.

When the phone rang, my heart stopped. It wasn't him. And again, it wasn't him. Now it was Amanda's grandmother. And then an idiot with nothing better to do than to call and warn us that we should fill the bathtub with water because the water supply would be cut at two o'clock. And then another fool called

Amanda's maid to tell her to meet him at the station across from the Cerro Santa Lucía.

Luciano never called.

That night I went home, and the next morning, when I went down for breakfast, my father was sitting at the kitchen table checking the results of the races at the Club Hípico. The newspaper was spread out in front of him, so I could see the opposite page, and there, like an arrow, was Luciano's beautiful face. I grabbed the paper. The previous day, while I had been circling around the phone, Luciano was robbing a tobacconist on Calle Diez de Julio. He had been arrested in a roundup during the late afternoon.

My relief at not being rejected or deceived by the above-mentioned Luciano was so great that it would have been the same to me had he spent the rest of his life in prison. I forgot him as quickly as I had fallen in love.

Thirty years had elapsed, and here I was with the same hole in my stomach and the same sense of excitement.

Early that morning—it was probably no later than eight—the phone rang and I jumped up. I didn't think Lionel would call so early, especially on a Sunday, but of course it had also seemed crazy to me the night before when he had the sangfroid to allude to our chance meeting on Calle Providencia in front of Clemente.

Justina answered the phone in the kitchen. . . . It was for me.

I picked up the receiver with a tremor in my gut.

It was Aunt Luisa, and she was crying. Her cousin Eulalia had died from a stroke at the Concepción Hospital. The hospital had just called. "They're all leaving me," she said, crying. "The worst thing about getting old isn't knowing you'll soon be gone, but seeing your friends go."

Doña Eulalia was one of those splendid old ladies for whom happiness was a question of social engineering. "I know I'm like a rebellious girl in an operetta," she used to say to my father, "and I know I'll end up regretting my romantic notions, but I can't live any other way!" She was a vocal member of the Communist party, and she liked to say that the party had given her more satisfactions in life than any man. Be that as it may, she was never interested in finding a husband. "Only a lesbian would compare the Communist party to a man," my father would say, erupting with laughter. Her pockets were always filled with useless objects: old screws; breadcrumbs; newspaper clippings; keys to unknown locks; and a crumpled, wilted old photograph that she liked to show to one and all. She would describe it as if it contained an important clue to her personality. It was one of those old portraits they used to take on the main square in small towns; this one had been taken in Curicó. In it, a young girl with an angelic face and blonde braids down to her waist stood next to a young boy of about fifteen, also blond, with the same eyes. There was a powerful resemblance, and it was obvious they were brother and sister. Eulalia would explain that one summer the boy had fallen in love with her and at the end of the summer holiday he had given her the photograph; she had kept it like a relic, not because of him, but because of his sister. . . . Clemente couldn't stand her. He said that it was fine to be a lesbian, but was it really necessary to brag about it? Her gravelly voice and compulsive smoking irritated him.

She had looked healthy a week ago at Aunt Luisa's. It seemed unbelievable: she was now in that strange place where memory disappears, having forgotten that the last thing she saw was the ceiling of a hospital room. . . .

Aunt Luisa sounded very upset by the news of her cousin's death. "I'd rather not come for lunch," she said. She wanted to be alone and read the last letters that Eulalia had sent her.

In the shower, I considered my own bad luck. I was (and am) obsessed with my illness. Why had this happened to me? Was I responsible in some way? I had heard somewhere that it is possible to generate a tumor through some sort of dark, self-destructive impulse. Some people think that breast tumors are more common in women who repress their feelings, who live their lives like open flowers for the world but shut tight to themselves, like an oyster. I had read that just as at one time people believed tuberculosis was caused by a consuming love or an excess of passion, in our day it was believed that cancer might be produced by the opposite: the absence of passion, an emptiness in the soul. In 1944, streptomycin was discovered and this crazy myth about tuberculosis was invalidated. The same will happen with the myths about this disease, I told myself as I felt warm water fall on my remaining breast. Even so, in the meantime, who knew how many women would endure this disease while feeling they were somehow responsible for it? These quacks added a sense of guilt to the suffering caused by the illness itself. I had to extricate myself from this web of myths and break free from the maddening need to explain my state. I had to avoid obsessive self-pity and stop thinking of my illness as a malevolent and invincible bird of prey engendered by me, and begin treating it simply as a disease that might be cured. I felt the time had come to prove to myself that even though I was as fragile as any woman facing the tremendous challenge of a breast tumor, I was also as capable as anyone of confronting the disease and seeking out the best treatments available to rid myself of it.

I came out of the shower determined not to continue seeing my illness as a kind of Trojan horse that would lead to the victory of the enemy within. We all have an enemy inside of us, a crouching monster lying in wait, ready to pounce when we least expect it, a dark twin that soaks up our soul like a sponge and absorbs all the miseries of life until finally one day it sets them all free.

Suddenly I was filled with a desire to live. Eulalia was lying on a gurney at the Concepción Hospital. But I was alive. My mother had climbed into death's carriage at a time when she could still have sent the dark horses back where they came from, without her. But I would not follow in her footsteps. I was here. I was still here. And I intended to hold onto this state—being here—with all my might.

After breakfast I went into the kitchen; I was planning to take a long time to prepare my pineapple cake, as long as it took for Lionel to call me. If I had stopped to think for a moment, this girlish attitude would have seemed so ridiculous that I would have said to hell with the cake and gone to the market to buy the sea urchins I had promised to prepare for Clemente. I would have forgotten the whole silly story. But I did not stop to think, and at no moment did I see myself as absurd or out of my element. I travelled back in time and experienced the nerves and whoosh of emotion I had felt at eighteen when I was waiting in Amanda's kitchen for Luciano to call.

Taking my time—Lionel might call in five minutes or at eight in the evening, or he might never call—I gathered the ingredients listed in Aunt Luisa's *Buena Mesa* cookbook: eight eggs, three cups of confectioners' sugar, three cups of flour mixed with baking powder, the pineapple I had bought the previous day at the market, and two cups of granulated sugar.

Beating egg whites is a meditative process. For three, four, five, even ten minutes, I repeated the same gesture, right to left, at a measured pace. The sound of the fork against the sides of the bowl reminded me of the pendulum of the Viennese clock Clemente had bought during his trip to Spain with Eliana Cortez. I remember the day I discovered he was cheating on me. I never expected it would happen in such a banal, unexceptional manner. One morning I called him in Madrid because a check had bounced and I needed to ask him to call his secretary so she could make a deposit into our account. I called the Hotel Miguel Ángel, where I knew he was staying, and the operator—it hadn't occurred to Clemente to ask her to tell any callers that he had already left for Paris or make up some other excuse—asked if I wouldn't like to speak to Mrs. Balmaceda. "Is she in the room?" I asked courteously, surprised by my own sangfroid. "Yes, she went up a while ago," the operator said, in her unmistakeable *madrileño* accent. I hung up. For a moment I couldn't breathe. What I felt must be very similar to what one feels after being stabbed—and I don't mean in a metaphoric sense. I felt something sharp, decisive, under the skin, different from anything else, something that froze the blood in my veins, stopped it in its tracks. Twenty years of marriage were torn to shreds by the operator's words: "Would you like to speak to Mrs. Balmaceda?" On this side of the ocean I was Mrs. Balmaceda, but on the other end of the line and the other side of the ocean it was not I but someone else. . . . I sat down, put two and two together, remembered details, made calculations, and discovered coincidences that had never occurred to me before, and the picture slowly became clear. After a while I was convinced that Clemente had been cheating on me for several months, probably since the day he had gone to a barbecue with Alberto in Colina. I had stayed home that day. I was tired. Clemente had returned very late, which was unusual, and for a few hours I had been worried. A lunchtime barbecue doesn't usually last until after midnight, and I couldn't call him because the house where he was had no telephone. When he came home I was relieved that he was all right, and I believed his story: Alberto's car had broken down at Huechuraba. But now, tying up the loose ends, pulling apart the little lies that had once seemed so irrelevant, and remembering his unexplained late arrivals, everything could be traced back to the barbecue in Colina.

One week after the phone call, Clemente returned from Spain with a Viennese clock he had bought at the Rastro flea market in Madrid. "I bought it for you because I thought of you every hour of my trip." Why did he say something so stupid, kitsch, and unnecessary, and most of all, so untrue? But the fact is that at that moment—and perhaps this is what kept me from hurling the clock in his face—I felt pity for him. I saw him as a mediocre man, a coward, half a man, I thought to myself with rage; he was like so many other husbands who go to Europe with their mistresses and come back with a present for their wives. And this was the man I had married; I had trusted in his loyalty, I had lived with him for twenty years, the best twenty years of my life, twenty unrecoverable years. But I said nothing. I never said a word about any of it. . . . As time went by I began to realize that the news of his affair had paralyzed me and the truth was—and still is—I did not know how to react. If I confronted him, I would be forced to leave and become part of that pathetic pack of women who have neither a profession nor economic autonomy, whose husbands have left them for another woman and whose only hope in life is to snag the first despicable man who comes their way, one who can maintain them. I chose to simply accept the situation; silence was the closest thing to pretending she didn't exist. And I loved him.

Two years later, I met her, or rather, we crossed paths and I observed her without her knowledge. I knew she was a nurse and that she worked at the Salvador Hospital. One morning I went there and asked for her. "Cardiology," a fat, gray-haired man in a stained white lab coat said. When I reached the department of cardiology, our paths crossed in one of the hallways. I read her name on the tag on her uniform: Eliana Cortez. I looked at her for a second. It was only an instant, but it was as if I had taken her photograph. She had pretty black eyes and an open face. She wore her hair back in a bow and she looked middle aged, older than me; I would have preferred her to be much younger, rather than my own age. She had a pretty, sensual mouth with a plump lower lip and very dark eyebrows that looked as if they were drawn with a pencil. In a certain, idiotic way, I felt power over her. I could go to the hospital whenever I wanted, stare at her, follow her, spy on her, and she had no idea who I was. . . . But I never went back. It made me so angry, those nights at ten o'clock when Clemente had not arrived, and then it was ten thirty, eleven, and he still wasn't home, and I knew he wasn't in a last-minute meeting or at an architectural conference, or seeing a client from Spain who had come to sign a contract. . . . I imagined her naked with Clemente. I hadn't gotten a good look at her body, but in that quick glance I had seen she was well built and slender, and during those long nights I would torture myself by imagining how lovely her back must be, and her long, shapely legs, her breasts, firmer than my own. Did she have smaller breasts than me? I imagined that they were firm and that when Clemente touched them her nipples became hard and her body wound around his and they fell to the ground, coiled around each other, and made love right there, on the carpet, and that afterward they would lie there and she would let her arm rest on Clemente's heaving chest.

I continued beating the egg whites until the meringue was about to pour over the side of the bowl, and then I stopped to take a break. From the meringue and from my thoughts. I was—and still am—irritated by this subject. Every time I think about them I want to scream. I remember what Amanda's younger sister Patricia said when she discovered her husband was cheating on her with a model from the publicity firm where she worked: "What I can't forgive is that he could do this to me after we had seven children together. If I didn't have children I would go out and find a lover, just to get back at him, to burn off my rage and the pain I feel. But who wants to get mixed up with the mother of seven children?" I didn't have children, but I had this illness. . . .

At eleven o'clock the phone rang and I picked it up, sensing it was Lionel. It was him.

"I owe you an explanation," said a gravelly voice, which I recognized immediately.

"What do you mean?"

"I think I do," Lionel said, dragging his words a bit.

We were silent for a moment. I tried to clear my mind.

"In any case, I'd like to see you," Lionel whispered, as if he were in a hurry.

"Why?"

"To explain myself."

"I'd like that."

"What: you'd like to see me, or you'd like to explain yourself?"

I smiled. He was flirting with me. No doubt about it. We were about to set off on some kind of mad voyage. This man, whom I barely knew, and I were on the edge of a precipice, about to jump into the void. I was sure of it. I could see it coming. It was crazy of me not to realize how dangerous this game could be, but now I ask myself whether it is possible to be of sound judgment when one is facing death. . . . Perhaps it is the only time in life when one is justified in losing one's mind. . . .

Lionel repeated the question.

I felt something in some deep, subterranean, unfathomable point in my soul; there was a change, a "click," a spilling over that made me feel light and blissful, free of dark thoughts, a different woman. I laughed, and as I heard myself laughing I realized it was a fresh, healthy sound. "Both," I said, and immediately I thought, "That's it! My goose is cooked! I've done it now!" and just in case Lionel hadn't heard, I repeated:

"Both. I also owe you an explanation, and I'd like to see you."

There was another short silence, barely a pause.

"Will you meet me at the bar on the first floor of the Sheraton, tomorrow at six?" he asked, as if he hadn't heard me.

I heard myself say: "All right, tomorrow at six at the bar on the first floor."

Once we said our good-byes and I hung up, I asked myself if it was really possible that I, Clemente Balmaceda's wife, Clara Griffin, had made an appointment to meet a man who was practically a stranger and with whom, it seemed almost certain, I would have an affair? Was I out of my mind? Of course I was. Soon, my world would end, memory would end, my chance to be happy would end, and so would everything that I knew, everything I had seen and felt; my pain would disappear, along with my prejudices, my mental blocks, my fears, and my friendships. Mornings would come to an end, as would the anger I felt toward my absent mother and her lack of concern for my life, and my inability to confront Clemente's disloyalty. I would take my good and bad memories with me, but I did not want to go to my death like the emperor Hadrian, with my eyes open and the sense that my small, vulnerable soul was floating in this new reality. I did not want to die. This was the only thing I was sure of. I have a terrible fear of dying. I don't want to go to that unknown place. I don't like the idea of being reduced to a memory in the minds of three or four people, like a sad story. The fact that I have no children is more painful than ever. Once I'm gone no part of me will live on, there will be no trace of me, and for Clemente my passing will in some way be a relief. His path with Eliana will be completely open. . . . Today I had trouble taking a shower; I almost fell, I felt weak and dizzy. When I looked at myself in the mirror, the sight of my skinny body made me pity myself. I was confused by the sight of those bones, that sagging flesh. I looked away as if I had seen a ghost.

{The Notebook}

*O*n March 5, the doctors removed Clara's uterus. Clemente could not bring himself to listen to the doctor's explanations. He was sorry that he had not been able to convince her not to let them operate right away. He had wanted to go to Houston first, to consider other options. He had wanted a second opinion. But the doctors told Clara that the operation might prolong her life a few years, and that was enough for her.

"I feel empty," she said when she regained consciousness, as if her uterus had contained the essence of her being.

Clemente spent ten days at her side in the hospital after the operation. He would return home late at night after Clara had fallen asleep. During this period he did not open the notebook. He felt that it would have been a betrayal, another betrayal, to read her words while she was still in the clinic. He waited for her to return.

One night in April—Clara had been home for a week and was able to get out of bed—he opened the notebook and found she had written another chapter. "She must write when I'm out of the house," he thought. He had never seen her with the notebook, and in fact he had never seen the notebook anywhere other than in that drawer in the kitchen. Her read the fifteen new pages slowly and as his eyes scanned Clara's pointy, neat handwriting he felt more and more surprised. He had no idea Clara could write so well. Her writing was fluid and made him want to keep reading, to know more. There was still something strange about all of this, something unreal that continued to surprise him. As far as he knew, Aunt Luisa did not have a cousin by the name of Eulalia. And if a close friend of hers had died in the past few months, he would have known about it. She came over for lunch almost every Sunday, and she usually spent at least one afternoon with them every week and stayed for dinner. She was one of the few people who knew that Clara was sick. In fact, she was the only family member who knew. This so-called Eulalia—a lesbian to boot—existed only in Clara's effervescent imagination. How could he "not stand" this aunt who didn't even exist? And why did Clara always have to make him look like a fool? He was the idiot of the story, the exasperating husband who approves of nothing and is irritated by everything, the mediocrity who is constantly shocked. It made him angry that she painted him this way, but even so he could not deny she had a fertile imagination, as well as a knack for storytelling. If he had not known the real story, this pile of lies would have seemed true. But the fact that Clara included so many details from her private life, and even worse, from his, made it difficult for him to simply accept this narrative as if it were a piece of fiction. It was a message. And at times, the message was a cruel one.

The trip to Spain with Eliana had really taken place. When he read that passage, his entire body shuddered. So this was how Clara had discovered the affair. And she had known for a long time. He had taken that trip when he was writing his book on Gaudí, toward the beginning of the affair. He had spent ten days in Barcelona and met Eliana in Madrid. It was also true he had bought the clock at the Rastro market and had taken it to Clara as a gift, but why had she made up the sappy line: "I bought it for you because I thought of you every hour of my trip." It was upsetting to be depicted as a fool. Only a fool would have uttered those sentimental words as he handed a gift to his wife, whom he was deceiving with another woman. . . . But what did he expect? How could he justify the way he felt? After all, she did not know he was reading the notebook. Even so, and despite the fact that she would never publish the book, he still felt offended by her words, and it was not easy for him to keep all of this to himself.

The barbecue in Colina was real. He could not understand how Clara had managed to figure out that his affair with Eliana began on that day. Other than his late arrival, there was nothing that could have alerted her to the fact that he had been with another woman. But she was not mistaken: that was the first night he and Eliana had slept together. And then there was Clara's visit to the hospital. . . . Clara had actually gone to the hospital to see Eliana. Eliana didn't know; she hadn't said anything to him. What he couldn't understand was how Clara had found out that Eliana worked at the Salvador Hospital and how she had discovered her name. Once again, he felt tricked by Clara, inferior to her, dominated by her. Clara seemed to know everything, as if she had a magic ball that told her everything about his life, his secrets.

Luciano was also real. Whenever they talked about their youth, Amanda always brought up that night at the Murciélago when Clara lost her head for a leftist who had killed a policeman the very next day during an assault on a bank branch, not a tobacconist. He refused to believe, however, that things at the Murciélago had gone the way Clara recounted them. He was surprised and a little bit shocked by the slightly vulgar, vaguely erotic language she used in parts of the notebook. Where had she come up with it? He reread a line: "What followed was a long preamble, an introit"—introit? Clara had never used such arcane language—"a glimpse of paradise; mumbled words, furtive kisses, a hand that touches the forearm and electrifies the body, a mouth next to the ear whispering something only half understood, the foretaste of a delicious morsel. . . ." He had trouble imagining his wife using this cheap, vulgar language.

He finished reading the chapter and realized that Luciano, the lesbian cousin, and Clara's other embellishments were of little importance. He was not particularly interested in Clara's inventions. He was completely focused on the story that lay beyond all of this, the marrow of her account, which was advancing slowly, day by day, moment by moment, from Saturday, October 9 to Sunday, October 10: the unequivocal account of Clara's affair with Lionel Hyde. He still thought it was hard to believe she had been capable of such a thing under the circumstances. He felt a sudden ache in his heart as he imagined Clara and her wasted body standing in front of this equally emaciated man. No, he could not imagine his wife naked in this man's bachelor pad. But the truth was that the notebook was the story of this affair. The rest was flying saucers, fripperies, a writer's flights of fancy. This story was what kept him riveted by the accursed notebook, obsessed by Clara's words. He had trouble recognizing that he was beside himself with jealousy, impotence, and a rage that he knew was absurd considering how sick Clara was. It filled him with pain as well, because despite the years, and despite his not always having been a faithful husband, and despite Eliana, despite all the things that one could hold against him, he was tremendously hurt that Clara had deceived him. And it made it even worse that she had done so when she was already sick. Now that he lived only for her, and gave her all of his support, and was careful not to abandon her even for a second and was always by her side, now that he kept a firm grip on her life and protected her, now she had chosen to do this? She had found solace with another man, a man whom she hardly knew and who could not possibly matter more to her than he did.

When Clara was in the clinic he had been tempted to call Alberto in Vienna to ask about Hyde, but a sense of propriety stopped him. What would he have asked? Whether Hyde was dead? Whether he had any news from Hyde? It would have been practically impossible to explain all of this over the phone. All he could do was wait for Clara to reach the end of her account. He would find the right moment to tell her that his affair with Eliana was over. He did want to tell her that, in any case. The previous night, they had a drink on the terrace, enveloped in the warm night air and the pleasant April twilight. He had felt light at heart and clearheaded because of the *pisco* sour and had the impulse to open up to Clara about Eliana, to tell her that for a long time he had been having an affair, but now it was over. He wanted her to know he had been afraid to tell her about it because he knew he was jeopardizing their marriage and was afraid of losing everything. He wanted her to know it hadn't been easy for him because he had never stopped loving her and their marriage still mattered to him. He wanted to tell her she had been a wonderful partner. And how sorry he was that he had not had the balls to be honest with her.

He did not know where to begin.

"How are you feeling?" he had asked her.

"Fine."

"I don't mean physically. How do you feel; are you happy? How do you feel about us, for example?"

He felt ridiculous. He blushed. He had never known how to say these things.

"I don't understand."

"It's been a long time since we talked about us," he said.

"Do we need to talk about us?"

"Well, I don't know. . . . It's always good to talk about what is going on with us, don't you think?"

"Do you want to tell me something?" Clara asked.

"No, not really, no."

"Go ahead, tell me. Is something wrong?"

He didn't have the courage.

MONDAY: RESTLESSNESS

*M*onday went by irritatingly slowly. There are moments when life becomes the hands of a clock; you go up and down the stairs and wander around the house, constantly checking the time, over and over. What anguish! It felt crazy to be in that state of expectancy, whoozy with nerves, at my age and in my circumstances. My illness must be affecting my ability to reason. I imagined different scenarios for what would happen later that afternoon at the Sheraton. First I thought I would tell Lionel right away that I was very sick and that none of this made sense. Then I decided not to say anything and to simply wait and see what he said. I considered calling Lionel's office, but I didn't have the number, and I didn't know where he worked. I could call Almarza—his number would be in the phone book—and reach him that way. I could tell him to forget it, that I had been thinking, or whatever other excuse I could come up with. But then I reasoned that if I called him I would seem ridiculous; what had I been thinking? Other than the lie he had told, which might mean nothing, nothing had happened between us. Absolutely nothing. If I called and said we should leave it, it would be like admitting that I had hoped something would happen. It was better to leave things as they were and see what happened. At no time in my forty-six years had I needed my mother so much. Who else can help you in such a situation? What would my father have thought? And my grandmother, what would she have said? I don't know how many times I checked the clock. The hours just didn't pass; that day was destined to go down in history as the longest day of my life.

At four in the afternoon I took a shower, sprayed on some perfume, put on my nicest dress, painted my toenails, checked to make sure there were no stray hairs on my legs, armpits, chin, or neck—after forty, hairs start poking out of the strangest places—put on the special bra that concealed my missing breast, brushed my hair carefully, applied makeup—paying attention to the eyes—checked myself in the mirror, found myself pretty, accepted myself, and left the house. I took a taxi because my legs were shaking.

I reached the Sheraton at five thirty, half an hour early. I went to the concierge's desk in the lobby. The concierge, whose bushy eyebrows fused together into one, was writing on a piece of paper. When he raised his eyes I told him my name and instructed him to let me know if anyone asked for me. I would be by the pool. "Absolutely, madam," he said coolly, and continued to write.

Years earlier, long before Clemente began his affair with Eliana, something odd had happened to me by the side of that pool. I was waiting for Clemente; we were planning to have dinner at the hotel, and I was killing time by walking around the pool just as I was doing now. Suddenly I heard a woman scream. I turned around and saw a couple at one of the tables, arguing so violently that it seemed they might come to blows at any moment. She looked especially livid. She was insulting him. "Liar, miserable wretch, bastard! Don't give me that. Do I look like an idiot to you? I don't care if they can hear me! Let them listen. Everyone should hear what a beast you are." I didn't know where to hide or what to do to avoid hearing them. I decided to stay where I was, and pretended to inspect a rosebush nearby.

The woman was beside herself. The man couldn't get a word in. It was easy to guess what they were fighting about. "I almost got on that plane, you idiot," she went on. "What if I had? I would have come to Washington and found you in bed with her! How could you be so shameless? She was there with you, don't deny it! Don't you dare deny it! Don't even think about denying it!" Now she's going to hit him, I thought to myself, feeling enormous pity for the couple. I don't know why men always get themselves into the same mess, or why a matter that should never go beyond the realm of secrecy and passion always ends up with a frenetic wife on the verge of killing her faithless husband and a pale man oozing regret from the bottom of his soul. We women must be terrifying. Or perhaps men are cowards. Or both.

A little later, after the man tried to open his mouth and she shut him up again with a flood of insults, the woman got up, probably to go to the bathroom and calm herself. As she walked by she fixed me with her wild eyes and said: "Mind your own business, you snoop!"

I felt my legs go limp and almost fell over. The husband, who had overheard from the table, came over:

"Please excuse her," he said, "she's very upset," and then he walked into the hotel.

As I remembered these events I couldn't stop thinking that now I was the other woman, the one in Washington, and that perhaps one day Blanca—whom I didn't
know—would scream at Lionel the same way. I looked
at my watch. It was a quarter to six. I fixed the curl
that always falls into my eyes, pulled out my compact,
and put on some lipstick. I looked healthy. It was a
good day. With this illness, the years cease to matter.
Your face can no longer be judged by its wrinkles, but
by its color.

The place was almost empty. A couple, probably
American, was sitting on yellow canvas chairs. They
were of a certain age. He looked like he might be nearly
eighty and she was not far behind, seventy-five or perhaps older. She had ordered a martini; he was drinking
a beer. They looked like they had been married their
whole lives, and it was probably true. They drank their
cocktails with that complacent look couples have when
they are content with themselves and the ghosts of yesterday, when there is no great hurry. They looked so
sure that all was well with the world; I felt envious. For
a while now, something strange had been happening to
me—or perhaps it was not so strange, considering my
illness. I no longer wanted to be young. I wanted to be
old, to reach eighty, to have experienced everything I

was meant to experience and to be prepared to leave this world with only the usual complaints. Like that elderly couple. I thought of Amanda and her American husband in Philadelphia. Amanda would probably grow old by his side, just like these two. Once they retired, they would travel around Latin America; Amanda would be constantly surprised by her own continent, and he would complain about our lack of punctuality and our dishonesty.

Pablo Milanés's voice floated up from a speaker hidden in the bushes. I remembered my father. "At my age, I would only marry a woman called Yolanda," he would say when he heard this song. The name of the writer twenty years his senior was Alicia.

At six I walked into the lobby. Lionel was there.

"How punctual you are," he said, kissing me on the cheek.

We went into the bar and Lionel chose a discreet table in the corner—he walked straight toward it as if he had reserved it—and we talked until nine o'clock.

I will try to reproduce our dialogue as faithfully as I can, partly because I want to leave a record of everything that happened and partly because I owe it to Lionel. I feel I need to account for every detail of the last days of his life. For better or worse, I am the only witness of his passage toward infinity. Despite the fact that I barely knew him, and was only beginning to build a relationship with him, it was I who was given this honor. It is an honor to be present at the most important moment of a person's life. Even if death is a solitary matter, as my grandmother said, it is still a great honor.

"What would you like to drink?" Lionel asked when one of the waiters approached solicitously.

"A martini," I said, perhaps thinking of the elderly American woman I had just seen on the terrace, or perhaps because it was my father's favorite drink. It was in fact the first time in my life I had ordered a martini.

"A martini for the lady and a glass of white wine for me," Lionel said.

"What wine would you prefer, Sir?" the waiter asked, with a slight inclination of the head that was almost a nod. It is a gesture typical of waiters who have been in the business for over twenty years.

"Any Santa Rita chardonnay will be fine," Lionel said.

The waiter went off and we remained silent. It was very dark, and I could hardly see Lionel's face. He pulled a lighter and a pack of cigarettes out of his jacket pocket and placed them on the table. He looked at me:

"I owe you an explanation," he said, abruptly. He cut straight to the chase, and I liked that.

"So do I," I murmured, and immediately felt I had said something meaningless, because the truth was I did not have anything to explain. Quite to the contrary, all of this was quite inexplicable: my naive schoolgirl attitude, the fact that I had agreed to meet him in this bar knowing full well we were not just going to play hopscotch. . . .

"Me first."

"All right. Go ahead."

"Saturday morning I was in Santiago, as you know, not in Punta Arenas. You must have wondered why I did not mention this to Blanca, my wife, and why I made no reference to the fact that you and I had seen each other earlier in the day. Isn't that so?"

"Yes," I said, smiling internally, but keeping a very serious countenance. "Why did you lie?"

"Lie is a big word. I didn't mean to lie. I didn't want anyone to know I was in Santiago. That was it. Let's just say I didn't tell the whole truth."

Again, he cut straight to the chase:

"About six months ago I started to feel ill, very ill. I couldn't sleep, I had terrible headaches, I threw up everything I ate. Some days I woke up with a fever, and I began to lose a lot of weight. I was always exhausted. Finally I had the courage to go to the doctor. I think that deep down I knew it was something serious. . . ."

"Cancer?" I asked, pronouncing that hated word limply, and as I said it I could feel it stick in my throat.

"How did you know?" Lionel asked, scrutinizing my face in the half-darkness.

"I'm so sorry, I didn't know, but those sound like some of the symptoms."

"Someone must have told you," he said, still staring into my face.

"No, I promise, no one told me anything."

"They found it right away. It was a tumor in my stomach. They operated. To tell the truth, they opened me up and then sewed me back up again. The tumor had already spread to my hipbone and was invading the aorta. There was not much they could do; in fact there was nothing they could do. The tumor was too big and had affected too many vital areas. They bombarded it with chemotherapy, literally. And they got rid of it. The doctors couldn't understand why I didn't lose my hair, but I didn't. I lost weight. A lot. Thirty pounds in a month. I became like a shadow. Now I feel much better. I've recovered relatively well, thank God. The doctors are more optimistic than I am, to tell you the truth. They think that maybe there will be no recurrence of the tumor. There have been other cases."

While he said this he was playing with the lighter and the pack of cigarettes. He flipped them around between his fingers, first the box, then the lighter. He lit the flame, and for a moment it illuminated his face, with its long bones and melancholy lines.

"I don't know where this disease is taking me. I hope it doesn't come back. But I think it is very unlikely. I'm ready for anything, I've resigned myself, at least that's what I try to believe, but sometimes I'm filled with rage, and other times I'm overwhelmed by a feeling of sadness. It suffocates me. I cry a lot. . . ."

He looked up, and I saw that his eyes were empty, almost expressionless, as if he were saying something learned by rote.

He went on:

"I don't want to drag you down with the story of my illness. I just want to explain why last Saturday morning I was on Calle Providencia, where you saw me, and not in Punta Arenas."

He took my hand fraternally, as if he were taking the hand of his best friend, and said:

"Blanca is my second wife. Before I married her I was married to another woman for seven years. We had a daughter, Cristina. When I fell in love with Blanca, it was very hard, very difficult for Teresa. I think she handled the situation very badly, but so did I. But in any case, we ended up separating and I married Blanca. Blanca was single, and she wanted children. You know how it is. I thought that I was desperately in love with her. At one time I was, or thought I was, but it didn't last. It's a long story, perhaps I'll tell it to you one day. Is this all too much?"

"No, please go on," I said, pulling my hand away.

"The doctor was very frank with me and now I am grateful to him for it, though I must confess that at first I thought it was brutal to be told, just like that, that I might die in a few months. It was like a door slamming shut. He told me I didn't have long to live. Perhaps six months, maybe ten, it all depended on whether the tumor came back. It's been almost a month, and I'm still here.

He was silent, as if he wanted to give me time to digest the bomb he had just dropped on me. The sounds of the bar around us disappeared into a void; I no longer heard the clinking of glasses or people laughing. It was as if the background noise had been swallowed by a funnel and trapped in a bottle.

This situation was not normal. It was much more dramatic than any of the scenarios I had imagined only a few hours earlier. I could never have imagined that this stranger, who looked like a younger version of Clemente, this man I had seen on Saturday morning, whose name turned out to be Lionel, would end up across from me in the semi-darkness of a hotel bar, telling me he suffered from the same illness that afflicted me. But there I was, in the bar at the Sheraton, sitting across from a man who just two hours earlier I had fantasized about making love to, and this man was telling me that he was hopelessly ill. No, none of this was normal. It wasn't the least bit normal, but the strangest thing was what happened next: instead of being horrified and frightened by the situation—we musn't forget I had not yet told my side of the story, I still needed to tell him that I was gravely ill, just as he was—instead of being upset by the proof that my situation was as bad as one could imagine, I felt perfectly calm. Suddenly all of this seemed immensely significant and completely logical. For the first time in months I felt that life was not a minefield through which we had to find our way until sooner or later an explosion would go off and our bodies would fly up into the air, torn into tiny fragments. Now there were solutions. I felt relaxed, almost happy, and instead of being paralyzed by the enormity of the news this man had just told me, I breathed deeply and felt all the nerves in my body relax.

"Go on," I said, taking his hand in mine, as if to give him the courage to speak confidently. I knew exactly what he was going through.

"When the doctor told me that I had so little time left, everything just went out of whack. I found myself in a tunnel without an exit. I didn't know what to do. The news was too big for me. I felt lost for weeks. I wanted to commit suicide; I never actually attempted it, but I thought about it all the time. One morning, everything changed. I went for a walk to try to put my thoughts in order, and suddenly I understood that the only way to live what was left of my life was to do exactly what I wanted to do. I felt in my heart that this was my only hope; I didn't have time or options. And on my return I told Blanca I wanted to leave Santiago for a few days. I told her I was going to Punta Arenas, I needed to be alone, away from everything, from work, the city, the noise, everything. One of my best friends lives in Punta Arenas, and I wanted to spend a few days away from her—I didn't tell her this, but that was what

I wanted. Blanca understood. She wasn't happy I was leaving at that moment, but she understood, and I was prepared to go whether she agreed or not. I considered going to Punta Arenas, I really did, and I even called my friend to tell him I was coming, but in the end I decided to stay in Santiago. You're going to laugh when I tell you this, but the fact is I have a terrible fear of flying. Isn't it ridiculous? Here I was, condemned to die, but I didn't want to take a plane because I was afraid it might crash. Anyway, I stayed in Santiago in a little apartment that Gustavo keeps on Tobalaba and Pocuro. Gustavo is an old friend; I explained the situation to him, and on Thursday I moved into his little apartment. It's not much of a place, it's a bit depressing, but it was an emergency. . . . And that's where I'm staying.

"Why didn't you tell Blanca?"

"Because I know her. If I had told her I was going to stay at Almarza's place she wouldn't have left me alone for a minute. She would have come to see me. She would have found any excuse to show up."

"But now you're back home. On Saturday, when you spoke to her on the phone, I heard you say you would be arriving late."

"Yes, that night I went home because supposedly I was arriving from Punta Arenas, but I had already decided to tell her that I wouldn't be staying. I told her everything: that I hadn't gone to Punta Arenas, that I'd stayed in Santiago, that I didn't want to come home until I had figured things out. Yesterday I went back to Almarza's place. I called you from there. I'm planning to stay there until I find something bigger, more appropriate. Almarza's place is very small; he only keeps it as a place to meet his mistress."

"Why did you tell Clemente that you would be arriving early because you were on your way back from Punta Arenas?"

"When I called him I was still planning to go to Punta Arenas."

Everything was much simpler than I had imagined.

Lionel tilted his head slightly, as if to indicate that he had said what he needed to say. We sat in silence.

So that's what he wanted to tell me, I thought to myself, still in a state of disbelief. He's sick and he's looking for a way out of the tunnel that his illness has pushed him into, the same tunnel I'm in. He doesn't know I'm sick; he thinks I am the picture of good health, and that I'm what he needs. This is what it was all about, it wasn't really about me in particular.

The silence dragged on. The bar, which just a moment before had seemed noisy and crowded, once again became an empty bubble in which only Lionel and I existed.

Lionel placed his hand closer to mine. I looked at him. He looked at me. How many love stories begin with that look. I've seen it in real life, in movies, in novels, and in Amanda's eyes when she told me that her American had looked at her this way one night in Philadelphia and how at that moment she had known she would go to bed with him. It's a look that differs from every other look that precedes it. Like a set of knuckles rapping softly on a door, begging to be let in.

"Shall we go?" Lionel said, fixing my eyes with his own.

I felt my soul sink to the floor. There was a violent trembling in my stomach. I was tempted to ask, "Where?" but I said nothing. I stayed still and in a fraction of a second the horror of my situation crossed my mind. I couldn't go with him, or rather I could, but what I couldn't do was remove my clothes in front of him without telling him my own truth, which was even worse than his. I felt, in a very physical way, the immensity of what was happening to me, of my terrible situation. I became acutely aware of the false hopes I had latched onto. Let's be frank, I was in no condition to start a love affair; I wasn't really in any condition to be meeting in this dark bar, drinking a martini with a stranger, wanting to make love to him. And now he was asking, "Shall we go?" and I was supposed to trot off like a lamb to slaughter, and remove my clothes in front of him and suffer to see how his eyes, which just a moment before had been filled with desire, examined the scar on my chest. . . . No, I couldn't go with him. Not before telling him the truth.

"There's a problem," I mumbled.

Lionel sat down again.

"What is it?"

In a voice that I can't describe to you—I couldn't hear myself—I told him everything. I told him about the terror that had filled me the night in the bathroom when I undressed and discovered that my right nipple was bleeding, but there was no scratch, this was blood from inside, strange blood that should not have been there and should not be coming out of that orifice. I pinched the nipple slightly and more blood came out, and then I felt myself go intensely pale, both inside and out. I told him about the fear of death that had seized me since then and never left me. I told him what I had felt when I was at the clinic, just before they took me into the operating room. They had left me on the gurney in a quiet, empty corridor next to a window, and

I knew that on the other side of the window there was probably a young boy crossing the street holding his mother's hand, a dog sniffing a trash can, two office workers smoking their first cigarette of the day on a corner, a young girl complaining to her older sister because she was walking too quickly, an old lady with her grandson waiting for the bus. . . . All these people, animals, and trees were on the other side of the window, each one of them living its life and unaware of the fact that on the other side of the window, in a corridor of the clinic, I was lying on this gurney, trembling from the cold, paralyzed with fear and distress. I told him about my operation. About the moment when I awoke from the anesthesia and knew instinctually—I didn't dare touch the spot—that they had removed my breast. I described what my breast was like when it still existed. I told him that the morning after the operation I felt so unwell, so upset, that I even considered writing a letter to my breast, a kind of farewell. I had lived with it for forty-six years, and it seemed wrong to simply let it go without a word, without a few sentences. It was as if I had been dumped somewhere without the slightest ceremony, like a thing that has lost its usefulness. I told him everything, almost without stopping for breath, because I was not only talking to him, but emptying myself out as well. I continued without stopping and without turning away, as if I were pouring my soul into the ocean.

When I had finished, he fixed me with tear-filled eyes that hurt me more than if he had slapped me in the face. His eyes were filled with compassion. Here was the compassion I so wanted to avoid. The promise of an amorous adventure that destiny had had the wisdom to concede to me so that I would feel whole, loved, desired, was disappearing, replaced by his sympathy for a poor sick woman. . . . This was what I had feared, but damn it, it was better than going off somewhere with him without saying a word.

"No, please, don't feel sorry for me, I beg you."

"Before I hang up I want to tell you something: I don't feel sorry for you," he said on the phone. But that was later. Now he simply took me by the hand and stood up and said "Let's go." He pulled some coins out of his pocket and left them on the table.

We went out into the street.

{The Notebook}

*C*lemente closed the notebook and shut his eyes. He was seized by a disturbing certainty. He was sure he could recite, almost word for word, what came next. He still had three or four chapters to go, but he knew that his wife had finished the story, not only because she had written the words "the end" on the last page, but because Clara was now very sick. She was slowly ebbing, getting worse each day. Clemente could see her burning down like a candle and he doubted that she still had the strength to write. The day before, she had woken up in a fit of restlessness, and when Clemente went to her she said that she had to go to the bathroom. Clemente brought her robe and slippers and she tried to get up, but she couldn't. She didn't have the strength.

"Help me."

Clemente picked her up with infinite care and cradled her against his chest. He carried her to the bathroom, and it felt like he was carrying a tiny new-born animal. She was so thin, my God, he sighed as he kissed her head. She was just a bundle of bones.

He put the notebook away in the kitchen drawer, determined to stop reading until later. Whatever happened, but later. Clara was dying. The doctor thought she had only a few weeks left. After Alberto returned from his trip around the world, twice Clemente had been on the verge of telling him everything. He wanted to ask about Hyde, if it was true that he was sick, if he had died; he wanted to tell Alberto about Clara's affair with Hyde. They had been friends for a long time, and Alberto was a strong person who would understand, but in the end he said nothing. His dogged refusal to share his secret sometimes made him angry with himself, but in the end he preferred to remain silent and not know what had happened to Hyde. He was afraid the story might be completely true and that he would not be able to hide his feelings from Clara. He had never mentioned the notebook and he wouldn't do it now. He didn't want to know the end of the story while Clara was still alive. He bridled at the idea of reading the passage in which his wife described her meeting with Hyde in Almarza's little apartment: Clara getting undressed and Hyde looking at the scar on her chest, Clara throwing herself in his arms and searching desperately for a way to forget her illness—or perhaps seeking something he had not given her in the past seven years—the two of them making love in the politician's secret lair. . . . The idea of reading about all of this made his blood freeze. . . .

He went upstairs and tiptoed into the room where Clara was dozing. She had spent the last few hours with her eyes half open, breathing slowly, moaning softly from time to time. The sound seemed to come from the bottom of her stomach, as if something very deep inside of her were in pain. It was like the sound of a small branch breaking in the wind. "She's breaking," Clemente thought, watching silently as life seeped out of her cheeks, her eyelids, her forehead, and her arms, which were so thin that they reminded him of an insect's legs.

It was the fourth of August and night was just starting to descend upon the city. Clemente went to the window and gazed back at the room; it was bathed in that warm, golden glow typical of late afternoons toward the end of winter. He looked outside and opened the window slightly to let in the cool air. He decided to go to Almarza's apartment. Somewhere in the notebook he had read it was on the corner of Tobalaba and Pocuro.

He knew the two buildings on that corner because years ago a friend of his had lived there. There was probably a doorman. He would ask in both buildings.

He went over to Clara. She seemed to be sleeping. He kissed her softly on the forehead and adjusted the sheet slightly.

It was cold outside. The sky was leaden, and the streets were emptier than usual. He was reminded of those dark, oppressive days during the Pinochet regime, just before the curfew siren, when people would scurry off, filled with the fear that on any corner a murder might be committed. There was not a soul in sight. Their house was in a very quiet neighborhood called La Reina, but it was more quiet and solitary than usual. He quickened his pace. There was a taxi stand two blocks away.

"Take me to the corner of Tobalaba and Pocuro," he said to the driver of the taxi he climbed into on the corner of Príncipe de Gales and Monseñor Edwards. That corner made him nervous; people said that General Contreras[4] used to live around there, in one of those houses, he wasn't sure which.

The taxi ride lasted fifteen minutes.

---

[4] General Manuel Contreras, former head of the DINA (*Dirección Nacional de Inteligencia*), Pinochet's secret police force.

"Do you know where Mr. Gustavo Almarza's apartment is?" he asked a man who was doing the crosswords in the foyer of one of the buildings.

"No one by that name lives here, but ask Señora Margarita at the newspaper stand, she knows everyone in the neighborhood."

Señora Margarita said that Don Gustavo Almarza's apartment was number 302 in the older building, the one directly behind her stand.

An old man of around seventy was dozing with his eyes closed and his head drooped to one side in a wicker chair just outside the front door.

"Excuse me, I'm looking for Mr. Almarza's apartment," Clemente said to the man.

"Would you like to visit?" the old man asked.

"Mr. Almarza?"

"He's not there. I meant the apartment. It's for sale."

"Yes, of course," Clemente said hurriedly. "Could I borrow the key?"

"Just a moment," the old man said, getting up with great effort and walking over to a table in a corner of the vestibule.

"Here you go," he said handing him two keys tied together with thread. "It's number 302. Please lock the door on your way out."

Clemente walked up the dark, cold stairway. The building had no elevator. It was one of those ugly, cheap constructions from the fifties. The walls were in terrible condition. They hadn't been painted in years. There was a dank smell of cooked cauliflower that reminded him of his mother's apartment, which Clara had described in the first pages of her notebook. He couldn't believe a sophisticated man like Almarza—for whom he had the greatest respect—would choose such an unpleasant and depressing place to meet with his mistress. A protester had scribbled "*militares*, you murderers, where are the *desaparecidos*?" and drawn a skull underneath. Farther along, and somewhat faded by time, he could make out the words "death to Pinochet."

He reached 302. There was a sacred heart on the door, and for a moment he thought the concierge had given him the wrong key. He put the key in the lock, nervous that he might be disturbing someone's household, but the door opened easily. As soon as he set one foot in the door he found himself in a tiny room, almost like a corridor, with a sofa and a glass table and nothing else. There was no space for anything else. Then there was a slightly larger bedroom, with a double bed covered with a pretty flowered quilt, two night stands and two lamps made out of bottles filled with pebbles. Then there was a minuscule bathroom and another space that functioned as a kitchen, with a gas burner and a small aluminum dishwasher.

Clemente sat down on the sofa. From there, he could see the bed where Clara and Hyde had made love. He looked up anxiously at the white ceiling. Somewhere in her notebook Clara had written that Lionel had died staring blankly at the white ceiling. How silly, he thought, that doesn't mean anything, almost all ceilings are white. He went into the bathroom and opened the medicine cabinet. It was empty. He went back to the bedroom. He lifted the flowered quilt. The bed was bare. The mattress looked relatively new and there were two folded blankets. He opened the drawers of the night stands. They were empty. He opened a door to what he guessed was a closet and was assaulted by the smell of mothballs. He crouched down and looked under the bed, feeling utterly foolish. What was he hoping to find in this apartment? Clara's shoes? It was unlikely he would find evidence of Clara and Hyde's lovemaking there. He found nothing.

He left the apartment, locking the door behind him. As he went down the stairs he met the concierge, who was on the way up.

"I was getting worried. The apartment is small. I was wondering what you could be doing up there for so long, so I decided to come up. Do you like it?"

"How much are they asking for it?" Clemente asked, buying some time so he could formulate the question he really wanted to ask.

"Ah, I don't know, you have to ask the agent, Señora Astorga. I can give you her number."

"Do you know why Almarza is selling?"

"I imagine it's because he hardly ever uses it."

"Was he the only one who used it?"

"There was also Mr. Hyde," the concierge said, and Clemente's heart jumped.

"Mr. Hyde?"

"Yes, do you know him?"

"I do," Clemente said. "He's a friend of mine. I didn't know he lived in such a tiny apartment."

"No, he didn't live here. He only came once in a while," the concierge said.

"Alone?"

"Yes, alone. He used it to rest. To read, he said. He was a very nice man. We always talked."

"Why do you speak about him in the past tense? Is he dead?"

"Not that I know of. But he hasn't been around lately."

"Did he mention that he's very ill?"

"Mr. Hyde? No, but now that you mention it, he didn't look well. He was pale and quite gaunt. One time I was about to ask him why he had lost so much weight, but then I figured I should mind my own business."

"Do you remember seeing him with a thin woman, not particularly tall, with short hair?" Clemente asked, and immediately wished he hadn't.

"No," the concierge answered, apparently giving the question no importance.

"I imagine you've worked here for a while."

"Twenty years, sir," he said proudly, "Pedro Rojas, at your service, you can ask anyone in the neighborhood about me, and they will tell you that I'm a fixture around here, like the bricks and mortar."

He smiled, showing a row of stained teeth.

"Is it possible to get into the building without your knowledge?"

"Yes, sir. First of all, there are two of us, one month Manuel, the other month me. We keep watch over both of these buildings. And secondly, the building has another entrance on Tobalaba. Sometimes I'm on this side, sometimes on the other side. . . ."

Clemente went out to the street. He felt he hadn't cleared up any of his doubts. But later, in the taxi back to La Reina, he realized that he now knew that Hyde had been living in the building. Almarza's apartment was small and depressing, just as Hyde had said, according to Clara's notebook. And the concierge confirmed that Hyde had lost weight, so he was probably sick. . . . Perhaps he had died and the concierge hadn't been told.

It was past ten o'clock when he got home. He went upstairs. Clara was still dozing, but she knew he had gone out because when he came over she said, "Where have you been?" Clemente was tempted to say, "I've been to Almarza's."

TUESDAY: WE MEET AGAIN

As we left the Sheraton I was overcome by an unpleasant feeling, as if I had just undressed in public. We went through the glass doors and suddenly found ourselves on the sidewalk waiting for a taxi. Lionel looked as if nothing serious had taken place. I didn't know what to say or what would happen next.

"I don't want Clemente to worry about you," Lionel said, taking my arm. "It's getting late. It's best if you go home before he thinks something has happened."

I stood there, stunned by his words. Why all this concern and solicitude for Clemente? He sounded like a benevolent uncle.

"I'll call you," he said kissing me on the cheek as he opened the door of a taxi that had stopped in front of us.

I don't remember getting in the cab or giving the driver my address. I felt clumsy and confused. It's best if you go home? I'll call you? That was it? I'll call you and that's it? When he had said "Let's go," I thought he was whisking me off for a romantic encounter, inviting me to go with him, to seal our meeting, to make love. . . . What a fool I was! Where had I gotten such an exotic idea? When he said "Let's go," he simply meant, "Let's go find a taxi so you can go home." That was it. And I had told him everything. . . . The whole song and dance, as Amanda would say. . . . What was wrong with me? How could I be so ridiculous? How could I tell a stranger everything about my illness, something I hadn't even told Amanda, my closest friend?

The taxi pulled out. I was a bundle of nerves. I was about to tell the driver to stop the car and go back to where Lionel was still waving so that I could tell him this had all been a mistake. But I didn't do it. "I'm going to La Reina," I said, and sank into the seat. My bed. That was all I wanted. A bed to lie down in and forget this episode that made me feel so ridiculous.

As I walked in the door I was greeted by a profound silence. My home felt like a sanctuary. Everything was steeped in half-darkness and there was not the slightest movement. Justina had gone out, and Clemente had not yet returned. I looked at the clock. Nine thirty. I was surprised he hadn't come home yet, because on Mondays he always arrived a little bit before eight so as not to miss his favorite political show on television. . . . A while later he called to let me know he was running late. He had stopped to have a drink with Alberto's brother. I felt relieved that he wouldn't be home for dinner. The first thing I would do was take a shower and then I would write a letter to Amanda. I had told a man I barely knew about my illness and now I felt obliged to tell her as well.

Dear Amanda:

I have bad news. I'm sorry to begin my letter this way, but I'd rather just say it: four months ago, one of my nipples began to bleed. The diagnosis wasn't good, or rather it was the worst possible diagnosis. I didn't tell you about this before because I didn't want to upset you so soon after your father's death, but I think that now I have to tell you. . . . They've removed my breast. They had to remove the whole breast because some ganglia were compromised, and I underwent an intense course of chemotherapy. I haven't lost my hair, but I'm so thin that it makes me feel sorry for myself, and there are days when I have almost no energy at all. We've reached the end of the first phase of treatment and I hope the cancer is gone for good. I'm scared, though, really scared. The worst thing was the mutilation. You can't imagine the horror I felt the first time I got up the courage to look at myself in the mirror. Amanda, seeing that horrible scar where my breast used to be was a terrible blow. I couldn't hold myself up; my legs just folded. It was as if I were looking at my own corpse. I couldn't even cry. I was in a state of shock. I closed my eyes but I could still see the angry red scar. One night I had a terrible nightmare: I was looking at myself in the mirror and suddenly worms started to come out of my skin. . . . It has been very difficult to accept what is happening to me; I know it will be a long, difficult process. . . . I've decided to tell you everything, just like this, without beating around the bush, because my illness is like this letter, an axe blow to the head. A lot has passed through my soul, my dear Amanda, since the moment I discovered that my body, this dear companion that has stood by me without complaints or surprises until just four months ago, is actually a cunning monster that will end up devouring me. I have felt in my own flesh how immensely fragile we all are, how we are just a pile of bones and blood. Someone once said that freedom is like the air we breathe: we only become aware of its existence when there is a rope around our neck. It's the same with life; I feel the rope around my neck. I've gone over my life in reverse, trying to understand things; I've tried to find God, to see if I can find consolation and a place to hide so I will be less afraid, or some space where I can imagine myself as something other than made of flesh and blood. I have sought a different dimension of life, perhaps happier than the one we live in. I've tried to understand the meaning of all of this. I imagine everyone does this when they are faced with death. . . . The truth is I've been analyzing my existence for as long as I can remember and I haven't been happy with what I've found. I want to believe but I can't. I want to find peace but I can't. I see breaches everywhere but I don't know how to fill them. I desperately seek some sort of spirituality but all I find is this pedestrian attachment to this goddamned life of ours. This makes me even more unhappy than my illness. I have not been what I wanted to be or done the things I wanted to do. And now I find it's too late for everything. I don't mean that I would have done things differently, because I know I wouldn't have, but even so I wonder what my life would have been like if someone had warned me when I was twenty that at forty-six I would be gravely ill, if I had known the exact sell-by date of my existence. Everything comes down to our limited awareness of our own vulnerability and to our ridiculous sense of immortality. . . .

Clemente has been an angel but I haven't been able to forgive him. He has stood by me through this painful litany of doctor's visits, hospitals, x-rays, poisonous drugs they in-

ject into your veins, and doctors who have the gall to express professional jealousy when your life is on the line. Would you believe that my doctor was unhappy when we decided to ask for a second opinion about the drug he was planning to use to attack the tumor? I hate them, Amanda; I hate the doctors as much as I hated the tumor that was embedded in my breast. I detest their incomprehensible language as well as the simpering attitude of the nurses, who treat you like a child: "Eat your soup, dear," "How are feeling this morning, sweetheart?" "Does it hurt, honey?" And there you are, lying on your back staring up at the ceiling, trying to come to terms with the idea of living with only one breast. My time in the clinic was the worst part of all this. I told Clemente that unless someone offers me a mathematically provable miracle, I refuse to go back to their luxury hotel where they charge you ten thousand dollars for an amputation and try to convince you that you are fortunate because you have the privilege of dying in a room with a view of the Andes and because there are fancy waiting rooms for your relatives, rather than the gloom and the stench of chloroform and blood at a public hospital. As if the fragrance of strawberries could guarantee you a better death.

I'll spare you the details of what my deformed body looks like, but I am happy to say I've grown used to the absence of my breast much more quickly than I would have imagined.

The process you go through between the moment when they say you will have a breast removed and when it actually happens is a curious one. At the beginning, when they explained they would have to remove the breast, I wanted it to be done immediately, completely. It was as if they told you that you have a plutonium bomb lodged next to your heart and that if they don't tear it out immediately you will explode. I thought that once the breast was gone I would be rid of the disease. That night at the clinic, when I regained consciousness, I felt differently. I was overwhelmed by a terrible feeling of loneliness; I felt that there was no one in the world who could understand this feeling of being the same person and at the same time someone completely different. It was like dying and then realizing that I had died, while at the same time being alive. . . . I don't know where my breast ended up or what they did with it, and I didn't dare ask. It must have gone somewhere, like the arms, legs, and livers of the soldiers in the Second World War. Lying there in that bed I felt like one of them. I remembered the movies where I had seen soldiers wrapped in bloody bandages with their stumps sticking out, their eyes lost in the horror of battle. But I'm being melodramatic; please forgive my exaggeration. I don't want you to worry too much. I have decided to confront this disease, to attack it, and to seek out the best treatment and stop feeling sorry for myself. If none of this works and I am doomed to die young, that's fine. But I'm not resigning myself yet. . . . I can't twist the arm of destiny, but I will not stop doing everything I can to fight it off.

I was just finishing the letter when the phone rang.

"Can I see you again tomorrow?"

Lionel's voice miraculously altered my state of mind. My pessimism disappeared and the colors of the world began to shine once again.

Yes, of course, but was he sure he wanted to see me again tomorrow, the schoolgirl asked? "Of course!" Lionel answered. "What do you think?"

"I thought that no one would ever look at me again," I said, regretting it instantly, but it was too late. I don't know how to explain how ridiculous I felt flirting with Lionel; I was embarrassed to be acting like an adolescent. I was a mature woman, almost old in fact, and sick to boot! All of this was ridiculous. Where had my good sense gone? How pathetic I must sound. . . .

"Well, you were wrong. I looked at you."

"Why?" I asked, genuinely curious.

"Because I've never seen a woman with eyes as sad as yours."

"And you like that?"

"It intrigues me."

That night before going to bed I inspected my face in the bathroom mirror. I wanted to see if my eyes were really as sad as Lionel said they were. From the depths of the mirror, my father's face emerged. He was saying something; I could see his lips moving, but I couldn't hear the words. I placed my forehead against the mirror and looked inward, tilting my head slightly to one side. And then I heard him singing his favorite aria:

> *I dreamt that I dwelt in marble halls,*
> *With vassals and serfs at my side,*
> *And of all who assembled within those walls,*
> *That I was the hope and the pride.*

He stopped, as if waiting for me to praise him for his singing, and then we both laughed. A moment later he disappeared into the mirror, leaving my soul to float in a strange place that belonged neither to this world nor to the next, but rather in the eternity of the moment. I felt a painful desire to live, to love, to discover new cultures, to learn things, to try to live my life again and reach old age transformed into another woman.

The following day, before leaving the house, I prepared myself as carefully as I had on the previous afternoon. We met at the same time and in the same hotel bar. But today everything would be different. We no longer needed to explain anything and there would be no drinks or interlocking glances at the bar. Now we would be dancing to a different tune, or at least that was what I thought.

I arrived half an hour early and walked around the pool. The elderly couple was there again, sitting at the same table. She was wearing a different dress, he had a new jacket, and today they were both drinking martinis. I smiled at them and they recognized me from the day before and returned my smile. The other tables were empty. Once again, I remembered the quarrelling couple. I wondered what had happened to them. That time, when I heard them fighting, I tried to come up with the woman's name but wasn't able to. When she passed by and scolded me for meddling, I saw she had a forgettable face, with anodyne and somewhat disagreeable features that could go with any name. Perhaps that was why her husband had gone to Washington with another woman, I thought, but immediately regretted it and reminded myself that I too had been betrayed . . . and the betrayal had caused me pain. What pain it had caused me! How many nights I had tossed and turned in bed knowing that at that very moment Clemente was with Eliana. Sometimes I stood in front of the bathroom mirror, lost in the attempt to uncover my faults.

I had to be flawed; somehow I had failed, I had done something to drive Clemente away. Was it something about me? Or was it simply the passing of time, which eventually turns every relationship into a boring habit? Did he find me predictable? Dull?

The night of the operation, when I awoke from the anesthesia knowing that my breast had been removed, my first thought was about the two of them. I imagined Eliana naked, beautiful, whole, and Clemente deriving pleasure from simply contemplating her body. Much later, I timidly reached one hand down to my bandages. . . . Now there was no way I would be able to attract Clemente, now I had truly become an undesirable monster. . . . From that night on, the image of Eliana Cortez making love with my husband acquired almost superhuman proportions; I saw her as a kind of mythological goddess as I, transformed into a fly, watched the two of them from a light bulb on the ceiling. I envied and hated her and cursed my own bad luck.

At six I went to the lobby. Lionel was there. When he saw me he opened his arms as if he had been waiting for me his whole life, and I took refuge there as if I too had been waiting my whole life for that place in which to hide. We embraced for a long time. I know all of this sounds sappy, and it is, but what can I do? These stories always sound sappy when one writes them. . . .

The trouble is, I'm a liar and always have been, ever since I was a child. My father called me "Pinocchia" because of all the lies I told. I kept track of them in my journal, which was filled with stories, none of which were true. My father read the diary as if it were a novel in installments. I must confess that things did not happen quite as I have recounted them here. We did not embrace for a long time in the middle of a lobby full of people coming and going with their suitcases and bags, looking surprised and checking their watches, as I would have liked. I suppose all love stories begin with a scene like this, with a sudden look, a passionate kiss, an embrace in a hotel lobby filled with strangers. In our case it was a kiss on the cheek, somewhat cold and conventional, like two good friends who meet by chance. . . .

We went outside and Lionel took me by the hand; I blushed and felt a slight nervousness. What was I doing taking this man's hand, in the glaring sunlight, in front of everyone, in a city that was like a small town?

We knew we were crossing over into a new dimension, the next dimension, the sphere of love. We didn't say when or how it would happen, and there was no need to. It was obvious that at some point we would end up in Almarza's little apartment. And we did end up there eventually. But that was much later. Now we walked around Calle El Cerro, talking nonstop. We had a few hours in which to squeeze our whole life stories. We were in a hurry; we did not have much time and we needed to get to know each other as quickly as possible, so we talked and talked, feeling the urgency of those who are condemned to die, and who know this is their last chance to say what they need to say. We talked about many things, but mostly about the past, about a time when we were happier and free of guilt. I told him about growing up in the country, when my mother was still alive, and he described his youth in Cauquenes. We were both *maulinos*, from the province that used to be called Maule before the military dictatorship turned the provinces into regions and changed their names to numbers. We talked about how I used to play in the fields of grass as a child because I had no brothers or sisters, and how he played with his five sisters who tormented him, and about his three-legged dog. I thought back to the time when I moved to Santiago, just after my mother's suicide, and fell silent for a moment; the afternoon light brought back the fragrance of the pines and eucalyptus of my childhood and the sweeping flight of the lapwings, who scared off the field mice with their screams. My father had arrived in Santiago a few days earlier to find a place to live and I had stayed on a few days with my aunt Luisa. When we left by train from the San Alfonso station, I caught a glimpse of the peak of the Trauco mountain topped by its scarf of clouds, and I knew I would not return to these richly colored lands where Enedina had hanged herself from the branch of a cypress tree. I told him about Enedina, whose face was full of silent sadness and who spent long afternoons in front of the stove waiting for the water to boil. But even when the kettle began to shake from the steam and heat, she didn't move. She never spoke. "I think she did not have a tongue," I said to Lionel, and told him about the night her husband Gilberto returned from town at dawn. Enedina had been waiting up for him. He came in drunk, smelling like a sweaty horse, just as day was breaking. He knocked over a chair, heaved a few incomprehensible curses, fell on the bed and slept for two days.

While he was still sleeping Enedina searched the pockets of his jacket and found a yellowing calendar photograph. Brigitte Bardot stared out, her fleshy lips slightly parted, grasping a cigarette in a long cigarette holder between her fingers. Enedina stared at her, amazed, at her delicate chin, her long neck, her round breasts, and then she crumpled the photograph in her hand, cutting the fleshy skin of her palm with her fingernails.

Before midnight, when the Southern Cross had shifted in the sky and the night owl had started sounding its dispirited call, Enedina went outside, carrying a rope and a wooden box. She walked toward the eucalyptus forest, just beyond the vineyards, and flung the rope over a branch of the only cypress tree in the forest.

The next day her daughter Francisca was out playing in the woods and found her. She sat there all day, watching her mother's body swing slightly in the breeze, and calling out softly, as if afraid to wake her, "Enedina, Enedina, Enedina"—she never called her "Mother"—but Enedina didn't answer.

Lionel listened to my story with rapt attention, and with this encouragement, I delved into my memories and my stories. After Enedina, I told him about the nights when my grandmother used to come into my room wearing her blue woolen cape, her feet barely touching the ground, and would wake me to say that the souls of the dead were out on the terrace dancing under the stars. I would shuffle out in my bare feet, still half asleep, and find only the quietude of the night, and no sign of dead souls. My grandmother was a liar just like me.

The clock struck eight.

"Shall we go?" he asked.

"Where?" I asked, my voice a whisper.

"Are you afraid?" he said.

"I don't know. It's the first time I've done something like this."

"If you're not sure, you don't have to," Lionel said. "I don't want to force you to go to Almarza's place. It's just that I can't think of any other place to be alone with you. . . . But it's true, it's late. . . . Look, Clara," he said after short pause, "nobody and nothing is pushing us. Why don't we each go our own way and meet on Saturday at Almarza's place?"

I was grateful. Tremendously grateful. Thinking back, I'm convinced that if we had gone to Almarza's place that night it would have been disastrous. Well, I have to correct myself, because the outcome could not have been more disastrous than it was. But all the same, it is true that I wasn't yet ready. I needed more time. For me, this wasn't simply about undressing in front of a man who I had only met a few days earlier, it was a matter of life and death. Mine, not Lionel's.

When night began to fall we went our separate ways. Lionel was traveling to Concepción the next day, and we agreed to meet on Saturday at six at Almarza's apartment. Clemente would be spending the night at Viña del Mar. The construction site there was a good excuse for all of us. Lionel wrote the address on a piece of paper and I climbed into a taxi, my mind in a state of confusion. During the entire drive home, I told myself that this whole story was a mess, "It makes no sense, what am I thinking? Have I gone crazy? Am I getting into an enormous muddle?" But none of this could compare with the enormity of death, so what did it matter? I had three days in which to change my mind. I could always call him in Concepción and tell him I wasn't coming. I would think of something; no one was forcing me. This was a crush, nothing more, a two–day–old crush, what was the big deal? "Calm down," I thought. "The world isn't going to come to an end over this."

{The Notebook}

It was Friday, the third of September. Clemente didn't know where the days had gone, how they had reached that date. Winter was coming to an end. One morning he woke up and Clara was much better. All of them, the doctors, and even Clara, felt renewed hope and crossed their fingers for the following three weeks. . . . Another day Clara had deteriorated to the point that it seemed she would not even make it through the morning. Clara's illness filled his hours and his mind, and the house was submerged in the silence that invades the rooms of the dying. The few people who came to visit floated through the hallways like ghosts. No one spoke. Amanda had arrived five days earlier and was constantly by her side. The day the doctors had said that Clara had only a few weeks left, Clemente had called her, and she arrived in Santiago two days later. It was a terrible blow. Amanda could not forgive Clara for not telling earlier. She had spoken with Clara several times that winter, and they had exchanged two or three letters, but she knew nothing about the illness, no one had told her anything, neither Clara, nor Aunt Luisa, nor Clemente. What was wrong with them? Did none of them realize how important it was for her to know? Clara had been a sister to her. But compared to the magnitude of what was happening now, what did this matter. . . .

Clemente went into the garden to smoke a cigarette. This wait—marking time for death to come—was tearing him apart. These past weeks his life with Clara had flashed through his mind with painful persistence, as if Clara's spirit were making a desperate attempt, in its agony, to impress itself indelibly in his memory. Bits and pieces returned to him again and again. He heard Clara's voice repeating phrases she often used, he saw her in different dresses, at different times of the year and in various moments of her life. He became aware of her vanilla fragrance, her long face, her well-drawn eyebrows, her hair. He remembered the things that surprised him about her, details he had not realized were so vividly marked in his memory. Scenes he thought were forgotten resurfaced, bringing back the Clara he had loved. . . . He remembered when she was very young and he had taken her to San Juan de Pirque, a beautiful spot near Santiago. That was where they had made love for the first time. It happened the week before they were married. They made love in the grass, and it had been beautiful, and somewhat unexpected. It happened without haste or pressure beneath a clear sky on a warm spring day. It felt as if they had been making love to each other their whole lives. Clara seemed accustomed to sex. Even though she was a virgin, she moved like a woman with experience, and Clemente attributed this to the education she had received from her father, who believed in free love, in sex without entanglements, in the sensuality of each gesture, of each juicy peach, as he liked to call his girlfriends. There was an abyss between the carefree, relaxed Clara he had seen that day and the Clara of the years that followed. She had changed, become more distant, more closed, more unattainable. She had lost the joyful spirit of the early days and turned inward, building a shell, protecting herself, hiding away from him. Perhaps it was a reaction to his betrayal, but no, the affair with Eliana had begun long after Clara set off on this voyage into her own impregnable world.

In the car on the way back to Santiago, after they had made love for the first time, she began to laugh softly, as if remembering a funny story. When he asked her what was so funny she covered her mouth to keep from laughing out loud, and then told him a story about her grandmother's Ukrainian friend who had fallen for a German woman. He was at a ball in Berlin and someone had introduced him to a very pretty, cheerful, uninhibited girl with whom he immediately hit it off. The Ukrainian asked her to dance, and the German girl, who was high-spirited and full of life, and gave off a fragrance of fresh-cut grass, swept across the dance floor as if the world belonged to her, completely happy and at ease. She pressed her right thigh against his leg and her body against his; every so often she would let go of his arms and do a turn, and then come back to him. This went on until he was half crazy with desire. They spent the entire evening together except for a few minutes when she went to powder her nose. Toward the end of the night the Ukrainian invited her to his apartment, and once they were there, after a few more drinks, he tried to make love to her but she tapped his nose as if he were a child and said, "No, my friend, out of the question." The poor man was in such a state that he tried to pull down her skirt, and she gave him such a punch he almost lost consciousness. It was then, when he was picking himself off of the floor, that he noticed something poking out beneath the skirt, pointing straight at him like a pole. He ran out of there just as he was, half dressed.

"Why did you remember that now?"

"Because a while ago I was tempted to put a carrot in my pants and play a trick on you," Clara said, laughing out loud.

Back then, Clara often laughed like this, wholeheartedly. She was light and free, like a feather.

But then she developed that absent expression. The same expression she had when she lost her child in the sixth month of pregnancy. When Clemente had come into the room at the clinic, he had found her sitting on the bed, with her big black eyes staring up at the ceiling as if her child were hiding somewhere among the light bulbs. He sat down next to her on the bed and caressed her hair.

"We'll try again," he said, even though he knew Clara would not be able to have another child. The doctor had already told him.

"There won't be another time," Clara murmured. She knew.

That was the only time they had discussed the matter. Clara had never mentioned it again. Now the lack of communication between them was so glaring that it made him want to cry. . . . He tried to remember a time when they had been able to speak openly to each other. Clara never told him how painful it had been to lose the only child she would ever carry. They never discussed adoption, for example. They simply closed the curtain and buried the subject. He found it difficult to understand why Clara had not made the slightest allusion to this loss in her notebook.

His mother had had a bad feeling about Clara from the start. She didn't like her. They were like water and oil. The day he had taken Clara to the apartment—the one that smelled of cauliflower, as Clara had written —his mother tried to make a good impression. She had been extremely welcoming and offered her a piece of the strudel she had made especially for her. But when Clara left, his mother said dryly, "I don't like the way she looks through people, as if she doesn't see them; I don't like that look of hers."

At the time Clemente was very much in love, and he interpreted his mother's words as the jealousy of a possessive mother—which she was. But throughout their life together he had seen "that look" in Clara's eyes many times. It was like a veil that kept you from knowing what was really going on in her mind.

On September third, for the first time, they had given her a small dose of morphine. Clemente was frightened. He knew that morphine sped up the process of dying, but it was not possible to wait any longer. Two nights earlier the pain had begun, and Clara's prolonged, deep moaning as her body disintegrated was unbearable. He could not let her suffer that way. Early that morning the nurse had come to give her an injection. Its effects were miraculous. Clemente was in the room; not even five minutes passed from the moment the liquid entered her veins before her face relaxed completely and a child-like expression appeared in her eyes.

"What a relief," she sighed. "It doesn't hurt at all."

Clemente had promised himself that he would no longer read the notebook, but later that day, when Amanda and Aunt Luisa went out for air and Clara was sleeping, he went down to the kitchen and pulled it out of the drawer. He found the chapter where he had left off, and saw the title, "Tuesday: We Meet Again." Clemente had already accepted the idea that Clara and that man had made love in the ugly, depressing apartment he had visited back in August, before Clara's turn for the worse. He had seen the double bed with the flowered quilt and the two nightstands, the two lamps, and the tiny bathroom where Clara had probably washed herself after the act. Poor Clara: if she thought that making love with a man who was as sick as she was amounted to a romantic escapade, it could only mean she had fully succumbed to her fear of death.

Clemente read on. When he reached the letter that Clara had written—but never sent—to Amanda, and read the words "Clemente has been an angel but I haven't been able to forgive him," he felt this was the real key to *A Week in October.* Clara had not forgiven him, and this was her way of telling him. This notebook was meant for him, and only for him. Now he could see it clearly and he was more afraid than ever of reaching the end. Clara had not forgiven him in all those years, and this was her revenge, the most terrible revenge she could have taken. He wanted to scream. . . . Now it seemed perfectly possible that Clara might have had an affair with a stranger. She knew he would find the notebook one day. She wanted him to find it. Otherwise she would not have left it in the only kitchen drawer Clemente sometimes opened, the one with the flashlight. But was she really so Machiavellian? He did not believe she was the kind of person who would think of revenge when she was dying. Perhaps it was the act of a desperate woman who, facing death, examines her life and, in her state of vulnerability, falls in love with another man? After all, Hyde was a decent man, a perfectly nice man, and he was as sick as she was, and perhaps they realized that they could help each other. Why not? Who was he to stop Clara from finding the help she needed? What moral authority did he have to demand fidelity from his wife? Was it not possible that his wife had truly fallen in love with Lionel Hyde?

It's possible, Clemente admitted, feeling a great wave of sadness.

Late that night he went into her room, afraid he would no longer be able to hide the fact that he had been reading the notebook. He thought that he would end up telling her that he knew what had happened between her and Lionel Hyde. He would beg her to tell him about it; he couldn't let her go like this, her heart filled with resentment. He felt the urge to confess his relationship with Eliana and to ask for her forgiveness. But it seemed so pointless to tell her this now; what good would it do?

The nurse sat knitting by the window. The house was filled with an oppressive silence. Somewhere, a cat howled at the stars. Clemente went over to Clara's bed. The small lamp illuminated her face, which was completely calm. She looked like a kind of ancient child, eternal and childlike at once. Death had already begun to leave its mark on her features. He kissed her warm forehead and stayed for a few moments, with his lips against her skin. Suddenly she opened her eyes and looked at him as if from a dream.

"How long have you been here?"

"Not long," Clemente answered.

"I feel better," Clara said, with a slight smile.

"Rest, don't tire yourself out," Clemente said, adjusting her pillow.

SATURDAY: DEATH

I practically flew up the three flights of stairs. I had the feeling that if I paused for even a moment I would turn back. I know myself; I am impetuous and my first impulse is always to let myself be carried by my emotions. But if I stopped to reflect for a moment . . . But I didn't pause.

I had spent the past few days fantasizing about this moment, imagining what it would be like, its colors, smells, sounds. I imagined the stairway, the lights, the sound of the doorbell, Lionel as he opened the door, and myself standing before him. We would embrace and then I would say something, or perhaps there would be a slightly uncomfortable pause. Perhaps I would not know what to do, whether I should throw myself in his arms or wait. How were these things supposed to work? I didn't want to seem ridiculous; perhaps I would smile, make some small gesture, say something like: "I'm here," or "Hello"? What was I supposed to say? And what would he say? Perhaps, "Come in, welcome," as he closed the door behind me. Then we would have crossed the bridge, we would be protected from the world in Almarza's little apartment. I wondered what the apartment was like. I had never been in a bachelor pad, as Amanda liked to refer to such places. One time she described the apartment where she had gone during a short affair. It looked like a dentist's office, with red vinyl furniture, a musty smell, and an ugly lamp that gave off a yellowish light, and just setting foot there made her want to cry. . . . But maybe Almarza's place wasn't as ugly as that. Maybe there was a window looking out onto the street through which the sun would come pouring in. Maybe it had a view of the mountains and wicker furniture, simple but tasteful and pretty. Maybe there was a silver ice bucket with a bottle of champagne and two crystal glasses and soft music, like in an American movie.

Wednesday, Thursday, and Friday I was filled with doubts and fears. Every so often I would pick up the phone, intending to reach Lionel in Concepción and call the whole thing off. Then I would change my mind and hang up. For three days I went in circles, doing unnecessary tasks, unable to concentrate on anything other than my appearance. I would look at my scar to see if it was as ugly and repulsive as I thought it was. I went to the hairdresser and had my hair trimmed. I went shopping to look for a dress and bought a bottle of perfume. On Thursday afternoon I drove out to Isla Negra thinking that the sea would calm my nerves, but as soon as I got there I drove back because I didn't even have the patience to look at the waves. At least I had killed three hours. . . . Now I was here, climbing the stairs, a transformed woman. I had spent more time applying my makeup, doing my hair, choosing my dress and shoes, and staring at myself in the mirror than all the time I had spent with Lionel put together. A burst of cold air came in through a broken windowpane. What an ugly place, I thought to myself. It smelled of poverty, of Singer sewing machines, of meatball soup, and it was dark, like a Russian prison. I went up another flight of stairs, my mind empty, and reached the third floor. Lionel had written the number 302 on the piece of paper he had given me. There were four doors on that floor. I stopped in front of 302; the eyes of Christ on the cross stared back at me. I checked the piece of paper and rang the doorbell before I could panic and heard his footsteps and the click of a light switch. Was he turning it on or off, I wondered?

The door opened.

"Hello," Lionel said, opening his arms calmly and naturally. I stood still, waiting for him to approach. Or at least I think that was what I was waiting for. Or was it that my legs were paralyzed?

We embraced.

I've written down in this notebook everything that happened, moment by moment, as if I were reliving the scene. This was all the time we had together. These were the last two hours of Lionel's life and the only two hours we had; these two hours marked the beginning and the end of our romance, the shortest romance ever known, a spark of what might have been, a preamble, a foretaste.

"Come in," he said as if there were actually some-place to go, which there wasn't, since Almarza's place was simply an elongated room—the living room, where we were standing—and another tiny, closet-like space with a bed and two night stands. There was also a tiny bathroom, and a gas stove. It was truly minuscule.

"This is it," Lionel said, guessing what I was thinking.

"I see," I said, taking in the two rooms, my head beginning to feel heavy.

"Sit down," Lionel said, pointing at the couch as he took my coat.

I didn't see an ice bucket or two glasses of champagne. There was no music. It was neither cold nor hot, and despite the fact that the curtains were open, there was no noise from the street below. I had the strange sensation of being stuck inside a shoebox.

We sat side by side on the couch. For a few seconds there was a profound silence, which enveloped us like a blanket. It wasn't an embarrassing silence, but it certainly felt odd. Now I wonder if it was the silence that comes just before death, but of course at the time it did not occur to me that death was lying in wait beneath the bed, like a hungry wolf. When I think of these moments I am once again filled with terror. We were living the last moments of Lionel's life, completely unaware of its presence in the room.

We took each other's hands, and I'm sure we said something, but I can no longer remember. But what I do remember is that it all seemed to make perfect sense, and the two of us felt much more at ease in the face of this loving intimacy than I could have imagined. The uncertainty I had carried with me disappeared as if by magic; all the doubts and fears that had tormented me over the past few days vanished, and I realized I was doing exactly what I needed to do. I had fallen in love with this man and he had fallen in love with me and that was all that mattered. I let myself be carried by that thought. I also remember feeling sorry for the two of us, for what we were, two sick people who had fallen in love, truly or perhaps in an act of extreme desperation—we would never know which. Two people who had given themselves blindly to a love with no future. On the other hand, it was not written anywhere that love had to have a future. The great love stories of the past often did not; in fact, many of them ended in death.

I think Lionel asked me if I was afraid and I'm sure I said no. "Come here," he said and pulled me toward him, and that was when we began to touch each other, to know each other, to see each other, to take hold of one another. I don't know when or how we began to remove our clothes, but there was no shame or embarrassment. Our movement flowed as if all of this were the most natural thing in the world. I was surprised by my own lack of restraint as well as his; I did not try to hide my scar or keep Lionel from touching it. My body disappeared, I gave in and became conscious only of Lionel. It was wonderful, unlike anything I had ever experienced with Clemente. Perhaps when death comes, love is also transformed. We explored each other's bodies with tenderness and time, endless time. I felt that it would go on forever, that anything could cease but this. What pleasure, what softness, how sweet his hands were; it was like floating in a beautiful liquid dream in which nothing could hurt me. The abyss that was awaiting us a few feet away had disappeared and the world was slow and silent, eternally silent; all I could hear was the sound of our steady breath.

We went to the other room. Lionel pulled away the covers, turned on the light, and we fell onto the bed, sinking into each other as if we were made of water.

Later, the telephone rang, but it was as if it were ringing on another planet, and we paid no more attention to it than we would have to the song of a cricket on the moon. We went on. . . . What a feeling of completeness. . . . At one point it occurred to me that I no longer cared if I died; I loved Lionel deeply for having given me a moment when death was less important than myself.

Afterward, we lay on the bed staring up at the ceiling, enveloped in the wordless torpor that comes after lovemaking, a feeling of being at one with the universe in which everything said and unsaid is contained in a relaxed smile. The little room was still submerged in complete silence. It was hard to believe that we were right above a noisy street. There was not the slightest sound.

Lionel lit a cigarette.

"How do you feel?" he asked.

I heard him breathe in the smoke. Now that I remember it, I think this was the last sound I heard him make. I didn't look at him, but I knew he was happy, serene, relaxed. I could feel his sense of calm. I smiled. I also felt happy.

"I feel good," I said. "I do, I feel good."

We stayed like that for a while, in silence. Many things crossed my mind as Lionel lay beside me. I thought about Clemente. Perhaps the hours he spent with Eliana were similar to what I had just experienced, and suddenly I understood him. I tried to remember what it was like when Clemente and I made love, in the days when we still made love, and I was unable to evoke those days. It was as if they never existed.

"It's strange how things happen," I said.

Lionel said nothing.

"Don't you think this is strange? Sometimes I wonder whether everything is preordained. What do you think? Perhaps the two of us were meant to spend these hours together making love. When I think about it, I get shivers. It would mean that all of this is predetermined and that there are no real choices in life. I would rather believe that, within certain limits, we are free to make decisions for ourselves and we control our own destinies. What do you think?"

No answer.

I had a terrible feeling of foreboding.

I turned to look at him and that was when I realized that something terrible had happened. Lionel was completely still, like a piece of marble. His eyes were fixed, very open, as if he had seen something that had shocked him. His pupils were dilated and unfocused; his face was pale, his forehead was tense, and his mouth was awkwardly open. My God. I shook him by the shoulders, "Lionel, what's wrong? Are you not feeling well? Say something, please, look at me, I'm right here!" But I was talking to a stone. "Lionel!" I cried out, upset, jumping out of the bed and dressing in a hurry. I covered him with the quilt. I didn't know what else to do. I stood in front of his body and stared at its shape under the covers. I shook him again. I opened his eyes, which I had closed before, and put my head against his chest. I searched for a pulse in his wrist, then his neck, and that was when I realized, with horror, that he was dead. He had expired just after we finished making love, practically in my arms, without saying a word or making a sound, like a bird flying away in silence. Suddenly Almarza's apartment became the darkest spot on the planet, and there I was, standing in the middle of that catastrophe, with a man who had been my lover for only a few hours and who now lay dead beside me. "I have to call the police," I thought, lifting the receiver. But as I was about to dial the number I stopped. What would I say? That I was calling from Senator Almarza's apartment to tell them my lover had just died from a heart attack? Almarza was a public figure. That was the apartment where he went to be with his mistress. His wife probably didn't even know he had a mistress. There would be a terrible scandal and I would have to testify. How would I explain my presence there? No one would believe my story. What if I called Blanca? It was ten o'clock at night. Calm down, calm down, I said to myself, and sat down on the sofa. From where I was, I could see the bump created by Lionel's feet under the quilt. I closed my eyes and tried to conjure a sense of calm. I opened the phone book that was on the floor and looked for Lionel's number. It wasn't listed. Neither was Almarza's. I went back to the little room and pulled down the quilt, leaving half of Lionel's torso exposed. I embraced his naked body; I could smell my fragrance on his chest. I was still there. . . .

I closed the curtains, straightened his head on the pillow, moved his hands from under the quilt and placed them on his chest, turned out the light, put on my coat, and went down the three floors, stiff with fear.

Once I was in the street I felt a wave of cold air. There was no one out and it was very dark. I walked to the corner to look for a taxi and then it occurred to me that perhaps I hadn't locked the door of the apartment. I turned around and ran up the three floors with my heart in my mouth. I had left the door unlocked. I went back inside and sat down for a moment on the sofa, trying to catch my breath.

I went out again and found a taxi on the corner.

Clemente wasn't home and Justina had gone to Rengo to visit her family. The house was quiet and empty, as always. I went up to my room and sat on the bed. I don't know how long I sat there with my head in my hands trying to put my thoughts in order. How could I have left Lionel lying there in that apartment? How much time would go by before Blanca or his daughter or one of their friends realized something was amiss and went to look for him? Blanca knew he was staying at Almarza's because Lionel had told her, but she also knew he wanted to be alone. She probably wouldn't pay him a visit on Sunday, but she might call on Monday, for example, and if no one answered she might think something was wrong. Lionel was sick, and Blanca would be worried and would go to the apartment and ask the doorman to let her in, and she would find him there. . . . What about his parents? Did he have parents? I knew he had several sisters. . . . In any case, the most logical thing was to try to find Almarza. I could also call Alberto López. Alberto was about to depart on a long trip around the world with his wife, but they weren't leaving until next week. I could call him for help. What would I say? That I had suddenly become his friend's lover and that his friend had died in the apartment where we had gone to make love, which belonged to a politician? It sounded awful, but what else could I say? That was exactly what had happened. Alberto would immediately tell Clemente, that was sure. They were good friends.

At about three in the morning I collapsed into a deep sleep.

The following day I woke up trembling on top of the covers. I looked at the time. It was eight in the morning. I took a shower and walked to Almarza's apartment without thinking about what I was doing. When I was in front of number 302 I realized I didn't have the key, I'd never had it. . . . There are times when life becomes absurd. I went to look for the concierge but there was no one there. I rang the bell of an apartment on the first floor and a woman who looked to be around forty opened the door suspiciously. "There's no concierge on Sundays; they both have the day off," she said reluctantly, and shut the door. I felt the die had been cast. I would tell no one, and the destiny of Lionel's body would have to decide itself. It felt almost grotesque, but there was nothing I could do; revealing my secret to everyone was worse. Everyone would suffer: Clemente, Blanca, and Lionel's daughter, and Almarza would find himself in an uncomfortable situation. No one would benefit from knowing that I had been with Lionel at the time of his death. Soon the story would appear in the newspaper: "Businessman found dead of a heart attack." It would not be the first time something like that happened; anyone could have a heart attack and die suddenly. Seeing that there was nothing I could do, I decided the best thing was to just keep quiet.

The rest of that day has disappeared from my memory. I have no recollection of where the hours went or what happened as they were passing by. I know I did not leave the house, and I think I did not even leave my room, and if pressed I would say I did not even leave my bed. I was paralyzed with fear, still shocked at what had happened just a few hours earlier.

As night fell I heard Clemente's key in the door and ran downstairs to embrace him. He must have found it strange. Such displays of affection were not at all frequent in our relationship, which had been dulled by the indifference that had built up over many years. What I felt at that moment was not affection but fear, but of course Clemente didn't know.

"What's wrong? Why this attack of tenderness?" he asked, amused and a bit surprised.

"Nothing, I was just waiting for you, that's all."

He did not notice the look on my face or my emotional state or the tremor in my voice, or the dark circles around my eyes. Or perhaps he noticed and chalked it all up to my illness.

On Monday, when I awoke, I asked Justina to buy the paper. Clemente was surprised. "There's nothing but soccer in the morning edition," he said. "Wait for the afternoon paper." I read each page carefully, my fingers trembling, overcome with uncontrollable nerves. Clemente sat next to me but noticed nothing.

One week later, after scouring the newspapers daily without finding a single word about Lionel's death, I went back to the building to ask the concierge if Mr. Hyde was home.

As I entered I saw a man of about fifty changing the light bulb. I approached him. "Hello, I'm looking for Mr. Hyde." I told him I needed to speak with him. I had called but there was no answer; I had knocked on the door but no one opened. It seemed odd. Mr. Hyde had specified I should come by at that time. Had he gone away?

"Don't you know what happened?" the man asked, looking at me closely.

"What do you mean?"

"Mr. Hyde had a heart attack on Saturday or Sunday, we're not sure. They found him on Monday afternoon. He was dead when the lady came in. She didn't have the key. She rang the bell for a long time but nothing happened, so I opened the door with a hook, and we found him there."

I felt my blood freeze. Everything around me went dark, and I was afraid I might fall over. I held onto the edge of the table, trying to conceal my nerves.

"Who was the lady?" I mumbled.

"Don Lionel's wife, Doña Blanca. She said she had tried to call him Monday morning but he didn't answer so she tried to locate the owner of the apartment, Mr. Almarza, but Mr. Almarza was away, so she came here with a young woman. It was terrible. Who knows how long the gentleman had been lying there."

"Did they take him away?"

"Of course. A medical examiner came, and some other people. They took him away that afternoon. I think they buried him on Tuesday. Poor Don Lionel, he was a very kind man. He spent last week in Mr. Almarza's apartment; he often used it, to rest. He said that in that apartment he could read quietly without being disturbed. Would you like to leave your card? Doña Blanca said if anyone asked for him they should leave their card."

"No, thank you. I'll call Blanca."

I started to walk aimlessly. I wandered around for several hours. Blanca must suspect that Lionel was not alone at the time of his death. Perhaps I had left something in the apartment that revealed the presence of a woman, and the family did not want a scandal. I still thought it was strange that Alberto had not called Clemente to tell him that his friend had died, but then I reconsidered. Why would he call him? Clemente barely knew Lionel, and that week Alberto and Clemente had hardly spoken because Alberto was busy planning his trip.

From that day on my life changed. It may sound
strange—what can change in the life of a person who
is condemned to die?—but I was not the same person
after Lionel's death. I owe a lot to him. I owe him love,
something I had wanted for many years to experience
again. I owe him emotions that I thought I had forgotten forever. I owe him a moment of plenitude, a moment in which I felt like a whole woman, with a life
ahead of me. But more than anything I owe to him the
manner in which I will face my own death. Lately I have
felt very tired. While I write this I feel my life ebbing.
I have almost no strength left. Yesterday I had to ask
Clemente to carry me to the bathroom. Today I had
trouble getting up; I don't know how I find the strength
to go down to the kitchen to finish this story.

Tomorrow, or the next day, I may be gone.

{The Notebook}

*C*lara died one day in September, in the mid-afternoon. She went in the middle of a dream. Clemente was with her. Suddenly she opened her eyes and saw everything for the last time. The branches of the walnut tree trembled in the wind, and one of them tapped the windowpane. On the dresser she could just make out her father's face peering at her from a photograph, and Clemente's face just beyond it, blurry and far away, as if he were somewhere else. Then she was enveloped by a still, blue night in which her body was weightless. She did not open her eyes again, nor did she say anything. Her forehead relaxed and she sank slowly into a slumber, as if she were sinking into a body of warm water.

They left her in the room overnight. Clemente told Justina not to allow anyone in. He asked Amanda to leave him alone with Clara. He wanted to talk to her, to keep her company in this last stretch of the journey. He sat next to her on the bed and took her cold hand in his and told her things he had not had the courage to tell her when she was alive. No one knew what he said to her that night. Only Clara knew. They stayed like that for many hours, as Clemente unburdened his heart and she assented in silence.

A week before her death, Clara had told Aunt Luisa that she wanted to be buried next to her father.

The funeral was simple and silent, like her parting. There were only a few people there, some relatives and her closest friends.

The night after the funeral Clemente woke up in tears. He went down to the kitchen. The house was steeped in a deep silence. He heard the call of a nocturnal cat who liked to climb the garden wall. He went out on the terrace. It had started to rain. A strange wind shook the branches of the laurel tree that Clara had planted in memory of her father. Next to the window hung the cow skull that Amanda had brought back from New Mexico. The hydrangea was in bloom again. It was as if nothing had changed, but everything had changed. A huge emptiness filled his soul.

He was watching the rain when he remembered the notebook. He went to the kitchen and found it in its usual place. He sat at the table with the notebook open to its final chapter. At first he looked at the letters almost without seeing them, and then he focused his vision and read, quickly. He needed to get through it, to know everything, to finish. When he reached the end he sighed deeply. Tears filled his eyes. He was in a state of shock. A deep sadness coursed through his veins, the same sadness he had carried with him throughout Clara's illness and which now seemed to fill his heart, threatening to spill over. Clara's words and the time she had spent with Lionel Hyde hurt him as nothing had before. It was not a pain caused by jealousy, but rather by his own mistakes, his guilt, his terrible sense of failure. He had failed. He had been a terrible husband. He had deceived her during most of their time together, lightly, without considering the consequences, without ever putting himself in her place. The notebook was a product of the great frustration Clara had felt. . . . Clara had to fall gravely ill for me to return to her, he thought, and the thought weighed heavily on him.

He let his gaze wander around the room, trying to grab hold of his emotions. What he had just read left him trembling. He went over the chapter once again, more slowly this time. He had been a fool and a coward. The affair between Clara and Hyde had probably occurred just as Clara described it. It seemed terrible that Lionel Hyde had died in such a way. A heart attack. There were such cases. He remembered his lanky, ungainly figure, sitting in front of the fireplace, talking to Clara.

It still seemed odd that neither Alberto nor anyone had mentioned what happened. One would have thought that people would talk about it, but perhaps it had not occurred to Alberto to bring it up. Why would he? If it weren't for Clara's notebook, Lionel Hyde would not have had the slightest importance in his life. He would have simply been a client, one of many. And perhaps his death had surprised no one; after all, he was already very ill. The only sure thing was that no one knew Clara had been with him. Clara . . . He still couldn't understand it. . . . How could she have gone through the final months of her life with that huge secret weighing on her, without saying a word? In a way, of course, she had told him. She had written it all in this notebook before dying. That was why she had made the effort to go down to the kitchen to finish her story. It must have been difficult, she was very weak. But in the end, Clara had confided in him. Perhaps she knew he was reading the notebook on the sly. Perhaps that was why she had left it in that drawer. . . .

He tried to go back in time and remember Clara last October, the Clara who had experienced these things, but he couldn't. The only image he could conjure was the wax angel that had lain on the bed upstairs.

". . . that was when we began to touch each other, to know each other, to see each other, to take hold of one another. I don't know when or how we began to remove our clothes, but there was no shame or embarrassment. Our movement flowed as if all of this were the most natural thing in the world. I was surprised by my own lack of restraint as well as his; I did not try to hide my scar or keep Lionel from touching it. My body disappeared, I gave in and became conscious only of Lionel. It was wonderful, unlike anything I had ever experienced with Clemente. Perhaps when death comes, love is also transformed. We explored each other's bodies with tenderness and time, endless time."

He felt a knot in his throat. He would never be able to erase that image from his mind. It was as if he had been there, spying on them. He could not go on reading. He started to cry.

In his wallet he had Lionel Hyde's number. He had carried it in his pocket for many months. One afternoon he had asked the secretary at Viña del Mar to give it to him. He knew that someday he would call the house and at that point the story would come to an end. Then he would throw away this little scrap of paper that cut him like the blade of a knife. He felt an almost childish fear each time he looked at the number. He had never had the courage to dial it. It was simple; he just had to press a few numbers and ask for Lionel Hyde, that was all, but he couldn't find the courage to do it.

He had a dream. It was the bottom of the ocean. Down there, far away, he could make out Clara and Hyde's bodies, naked, floating around each other, coming close, smelling each other, floating away, each caressing the other's scaly skin with its tail. It was like a dance; their tails went up and down, forming eddies of dark water that made it difficult to see. Their heads were attached to two silvery fish bodies. They looked at him and smiled childishly, as if they were playing a game.

When he awoke the dream was still vivid, hovering between his eyebrows. As if an outside force were guiding his hand, he pulled his wallet out of the drawer of the night stand and looked for the little paper with Hyde's number on it.

"Could I please speak with Lionel Hyde?" he asked, still half-submerged in the dream.

"He's not at home right now," a woman's voice said.

There was a short pause.

"Do you know when he will return?"

"He went to buy cigarettes around the corner, so he shouldn't be more than a few minutes. Would you like to leave a message?"

"No thank you. I'll call back later."